"A light shines in the darkness,
and the darkness has not overcome it."
John 1:5 NIV

THE CHRONICLE OF THE THREE: EDEN SWORD

TABITHA CAPLINGER

BLUE INK
PRESS

Published by Blue Ink Press, LLC

Printed in the United States of America

Cover design by Greg Simanson

ISBN-13: 978-1-948449-02-1

ISBN-10: 1-948449-02-1

Library of Congress Control Number: 2018937443

www.blueinkpress.com

For the demon slayers:
Keep fighting the shadows;
Keep looking for the light;
Keep living chosen;
Keep saving the world.

CHAPTER ONE

Zoe watched Lucas's peaceful smile dim, his life drifting away on the Maker's warm wind as his body fell forward into the blood-covered snow. The hellhounds and shadows had all dissolved into ashes, leaving only the cold of the December snow, which was still falling in light, glittering flakes. Tears dripped in warm lines down Zoe's chilled cheeks. She dropped to her knees next to Lucas, pulled him up into her shaking arms, and clung to his limp, lifeless body.

"No, no, no..." Zoe muttered the word over and over as if the chant would change something. Footsteps crunched in the fresh snow around her. She glanced up to find Daniel, Claire, and Michael looking down at her. Their eyes were heavy with shock, their faces streaked with sadness. Bitterness rose to the back of her throat and she swallowed it down, once again burying her head into the crook of Lucas's neck, weeping and praying for this to be just another nightmare.

* * *

Abaddon stared at the marred face of his alter ego in the dingy mirror as Meredith's reflection came into view behind him.

"They have the map, and we didn't kill Claire," Meredith snapped as she wiped the blood from her neck with a cloth.

"Merely a small setback." Abaddon watched new skin grow from the singes covering his black, stone face. "Killing that boy will have to do for now."

"But is it enough now that they have the map?" Meredith asked.

"Don't you trust me?" Abaddon asked as he turned to her, took a step closer, and reached a threatening hand toward her.

She cringed. "I...uh...of course I do."

The beast paused. "Good girl," he said, smirking. He used his thumb to wipe a drop of blood from the corner of her lips. "Don't fear, love. Things may not have gone exactly according to our plan. The Armor-Bearer lives, but the Daughter *is* frail. She hadn't even realized her full strength before she started to weaken."

Meredith looked downward as she asked, "And when she realizes it?"

Abaddon grabbed her face, forcing her gaze toward him. "We will have to keep that from happening"—he squeezed a little tighter before he released her—"won't we?"

* * *

The sun was just a sliver of faint light drowning on the horizon when Maggie stepped into the dimly lit barn. "Can no one text a girl back?" she asked, her jovial tone matching the lightness of her heart. *They're alive.* But her relief was crushed when she saw what appeared to be a body lying on the training mat underneath a dusty blanket. The others were huddled around the covered corpse, heads bowed, barely making an effort to look her in the eyes.

"What happened?" Maggie's voice choked out of her tightening throat.

Claire stood at the corpse's feet with her arm clutched against her side. Was it broken? Could Claire even break?

Claire's eyes were dull and wet as she turned slowly away from the body. "Mags...something happened...Lucas didn't..." She struggled to get the words out.

"No," Maggie gasped. "He can't be..."

"He is." Claire's eyebrows were pinched together. She reached her good arm out and pulled Maggie into her embrace.

Maggie peeked over Claire's shoulder, trying to gain some understanding from the others, some hint that this wasn't what she thought. Daniel was squatted on the floor, elbows resting on his knees, face held in his hands. Garrett leaned against a pole, his jaw tight and eyes bloodshot. Even Michael seemed forlorn standing over the body. Zoe was just staring into the dark corners of the barn, no sign of life in her eyes, as if it had drained out of her and left with Lucas's. Then Maggie returned her attention to the old Navajo blanket that covered her friend. Was he just a friend or had he started to become more? She couldn't stop herself from wondering, as if it even mattered now. Her eyes traced the pattern of lines and colors on the blanket from one end to the other as she surveyed the curves that were Lucas's head and shoulders. She stared hard at the line of his chest, waiting for it to rise and fall, to tell them this was all some cruel mistake and he would be fine. When it hurt to wait for that hope any longer, she let her gaze continue down the blanket to find his blood-stained black converse peeking out from under the fabric's weave. That sight made this all too real. Her stomach turned and she choked back vomit. Hot tears stung her cheeks. A pain started in her head and reverberated through her limbs, making her feel weak and dizzy. She gripped Claire's jacket and felt the woman's arm tighten around her shoulder. A guttural scream pierced through the quiet. Claire pulled her tighter and Maggie realized the cry had been her own. She swallowed down another as she buried her head against Claire.

* * *

At some point—she had no idea how long it had taken—Zoe rejoined the living. The sounds of stifled sobs and sad questions found their way inside her ears. Perhaps it had been Maggie's screams that had forced her return? They had started as just a muffled noise, like the static of an untuned radio but became clearer as she blinked her dry eyes into focus and took in the scene around her. Daniel was sitting next to her, holding her hand. When had he taken her hand? She hadn't even felt him touch her. Maggie was on her knees next to Lucas's body, her hands trembling like she wanted to touch him but was afraid to. Claire stood in the doorway, staring out into the darkness. Michael and Garrett were by Claire's side.

"What will we tell people?" Claire asked.

Zoe inclined her head at her aunt's words. A couple of months ago, no one would have noticed Lucas being gone. Even the school would have probably assumed him a runaway and not given a second thought to his sudden absence. But now...now he had friends and he was making good grades and...what *would* they tell people? Why did they even care about the rest of the world? Did it matter? A part of their family was gone—like a limb suddenly severed—and they were worried about other people?

Zoe stood up, her body shaking. "We won't have to tell them anything," she announced.

Claire and Garrett both turned, staring at her with tilted heads and narrowed eyes.

"Just bring him back and it won't matter. We won't need a story," Zoe told Michael. "Just bring him back like you did my dad."

Michael turned and looked at her with eyes full of pity. "I cannot," he replied.

His words weren't as cool as normal, but they still pricked at her heart painfully and drew out an anger she couldn't hold back. "What do you mean you can't? If you did it before, you can do it again. It's simple!"

"Zoe—" Garrett began to walk toward her but stopped when she held up a hand and started her own short trek to the Guardian. "It is not so simple, Zoe," Michael explained. "I am afraid it was difficult enough to bring your father through the veil. Unless the Maker chooses to bring Lucas back Himself, it would be impossible."

Zoe stopped midstep. It was like she hit an invisible force and couldn't move any further. The anger was still there but now displaced, and she didn't know what to do with it. She glanced around the room. Daniel had stood and was watching her with soft eyes. She knew he was waiting for her to tell him what she needed. She only wished she knew what that was.

Maggie was staring at her, her lip quivering, begging her friend for something, but Zoe had nothing to offer her right then. Claire and Garrett also looked at her with the same sympathy she had seen in the angel. Fresh tears tried to rise from some well so deep inside her that she hadn't even known it was there. A tremble followed from the same deep place and turned into words she didn't want to hear. "We were supposed to save him."

Michael took a step toward her. "But he was saved."

"He's dead," Zoe said. "We watched him die bleeding in that snow. How was that saving him?" She wrapped her arms around herself to either to fight off the sudden chill or to keep from falling further apart. She didn't know which, really.

Michael took another step and touched his hands to her shoulders, looking down into her blurry eyes. "Do you not see? He sacrificed himself for Claire. For you. He had changed. The Maker was there with him. There was no more pain or regret waiting for him. Yes, Lucas died, and that cannot be undone...but he died free."

Zoe listened to the words that she knew were true, and yet, she could not *feel* the truth in them. It didn't reach her heart, though she could sense it fighting its way there. She drew in a sharp breath, trying to help it move into that deep well, but it was forced back out with a sob. She lowered her head into Michael's chest and cried. She felt the Guardian's arms wrap around her. Then she felt new arms pull her close and could smell her father's familiar aftershave. The chill of the winter air was now blocked by her family surrounding her. Life was coming back into her bones, but with it came pain, and this time she was unsure she could win against it.

CHAPTER TWO

Alex could feel his skin burning from the heat of the afternoon sun. He blinked against its brightness. He heard Claire calling his name, but she was nowhere to be seen in the abandoned marketplace. He spun on his heels, continuing his search for her, but found only the nightmarish demons of his demise slinking atop broken carts and overturned tables. They hissed, and he could feel the air chill around him. They scratched their claws on their perches, and his heart quickened.

"It's not real," he closed his eyes and whispered. The air got colder and tickled the back of his neck.

"Of course it's real, Alex."

Alex squeezed his eyes tighter before opening them to find Abaddon standing in front of him, his head tilted casually.

"But, I know what you meant and you're right. This is just a dream, an invasion of your mind." Abaddon circled around him. "Sorry for the intrusion by the way, but make no mistake, I can just as easily kill you here as I did...well...here. But I don't want to kill you this time." The Destroyer's face curled into a sick smile.

"What *do* you want?"

7

"I want to help you," Abaddon answered. "It's what I've always wanted. To give you your life back, remember?"

Alex pressed his nails into his palms. "No, you want me to betray the people I love."

"*Person*. The person you love," Abaddon corrected. "Let's not pretend you really care about the others. It is Claire you love, and the rest of them are just baggage you know she won't leave behind."

"That's not true."

"Are you sure?" Abaddon squinted his black eyes. "I mean, if Claire were gone, would you stick around to take care of poor little Zoe? Do you really care what happens to Daniel or sweet, sweet Maggie? I mean, you're sitting in the hospital by the bedside of an old man you don't even really like. Why? Because Claire asked you to. Because it matters to her, and *you* want to matter to her."

"I *do* matter," Alex declared. His muscles pulled tight from his jaw down through his shoulders and all the way to his still-clenched fists. "Claire loves me."

"She used to love you," Abaddon continued. "Now you're just a distraction. A complication."

"You're a liar." But Alex could hear the jitter in his own voice as he spoke.

"Am I? Look, I'm not here to hurt you. Like I said, I want to help you."

Alex relaxed his hands. "How can you help me? You can't make Claire love me again."

Abaddon pursed his lips and shook his head slowly. "No, I can't," he said, then flashed Alex another smile, one that was small and almost innocent. "But I can get rid of the obstacles."

"What do you mean?" Alex regretted the question the moment he asked it, but he couldn't help himself. He was so desperate for any bits of hope offered to him, even if it was a dangerous hope. He shouldn't trust Abaddon. Can you *trust* evil? Did it matter now? He was losing sight of any other options to keep Claire close to him, so even this risky trust, this dangerous hope, was better than the void his life would be without her. Perhaps this alliance, a minor indiscretion, would be worth it? Could it hurt to examine it further?

Abaddon turned his back and walked toward the shade of a ripped awning. "If this whole prophecy war to end all wars were over, then there would be nothing standing in your way. Claire wouldn't have so much weighing on her. She would have room for you again."

"But it isn't just this war..." Alex began, jealousy twisting inside his chest.

Abaddon stopped and looked back over his shoulder. "You fear her feelings for the Guardian. The angel is only here to help the Armor-Bearer and the Daughter. When they no longer need his help, he will have to leave. Assuming he survives."

Alex took three small steps toward the Destroyer. "What are you offering, exactly?"

"We all really want the same thing, Alex—for this to be over. We can help each other, you and I. You want to win Claire's heart, and I can give you the power to do it."

"And in return?"

"Help me finish this."

Alex pulled back. "Finishing this means Zoe will die?"

"The girl will most likely die no matter what."

"I won't help you kill anyone." Alex began to step backward toward retreat when the shadows surrounding him screeched. He hadn't realized they'd been closing in on him, and now he couldn't move through the darkness that pressed against him, its coldness stinging his bare arms and neck.

"Dear boy, you no longer have a choice. You have played too close to the line. Your fears are too hungry for you to fight them now. It is this or death."

Icy claws scratched through Alex's shirt and tore his skin. He wanted Claire; more than anything, he wanted her to love him again. He wanted them to go back to the way things had been before this supernatural reality had collided with his world. The two had collided though, they had crashed together in pain and fear and love and hope and regret. None of that could be undone, but he didn't want to make it worse. He wanted Claire but not like this. He couldn't do this...could he? No, he would rather die himself than be part of her feeling pain. He bit back against his own pain. "I choose death," he said, the words pushing through his gritted teeth. The demon's claws dug deeper and burned through his flesh and into his bones. He could feel his strength drain, and in weakness he dropped his head and whispered, "I want to choose death."

Abaddon laughed. "You aren't that noble, Alex. Selfishness brought you back, and it will keep you here now. Stop fighting it. The only purpose that serves is to keep you from what you want. Accept my help."

* * *

Alex heard his name. Was it Claire? He felt her breath as she whispered into his ear and then her hand nudged his arm. "Alex," Claire whispered again.

Alex shook his head and sat up, wiping his tired eyes with the bottoms of his palms. As sleep and the voices from his dreams exited his mind, his awareness of reality flooded back in. The room was dim, the machines connected to Charlie were still beeping their monotonous rhythm, and Claire was standing beside him, watching him, her expression anguished. "What happened?" he asked and stood up.

Claire opened her mouth to speak but no words formed, her only answer the tears that pooled in her tired eyes. Alex reached out to embrace her but she winced at the contact, and only then did he take notice of the way she tenderly held her arm.

"I think I forgot it was broken," she said. A weak smile pushed upward just enough that the tears spilled over her lashes.

"How could you forget a broken arm?" Alex asked. He reached for her again, wiping her damp cheeks with his thumbs.

"The pain of the arm paled in comparison to everything else," she said.

"What else, Claire?"

"Can we talk about it in the car?"

Alex nodded. "What about your arm?"

Claire regarded her injury and then looked back up with a more relaxed expression. "Michael will take care of it."

The familiar coiling tightened around Alex's ribcage. He grabbed his jacket off the back of the chair and followed Claire without another word.

CHAPTER THREE

Six days. That's how long it had been since the first snow of winter, since silence filled too many hours, since Lucas had gone. Plans and excuses had been made and an empty body was buried quietly near the burned-out farmhouse.

Zoe had barely been aware of most of it. She walked through it, a ghostly apparition, silent and shallow. They had all tried to comfort her, to encourage her to be strong, to fight, but she couldn't muster the will. Instead she curled herself into her blankets and stared at the gray winter sky fading into night outside her window.

* * *

Zoe blinked her eyes open to the vision inside her mind. Her peaceful field had long been lost to the smoldering war zone before her. Ashes rose from dying embers as shadows hissed over the dead. The air smelled bitter and stung her nose.

"It's lovely, isn't it?"

She knew it was Abaddon lurking behind her and squeezed

her fingers into fists. "After a week, it's actually getting a little predictable. I think you can do better," she said.

"How about this?"

Zoe heard the hiss of shadows that answered the snap of Abaddon's fingers. She turned to see the Destroyer kneeling over a fresh corpse, his rocky fingers brushing a hair from its face. It was Lucas. Zoe's chest constricted around her heart and squeezed until she could barely breathe.

Her adversary stood and said, "It's sad that he had to die. Well, he didn't *have* to. But I told you they would all die. He just got to be first. How lucky." The Beast's mouth curled to reveal his obsidian fangs.

"Shut up," Zoe said, trying to conceal the tremble of her bottom lip with a false courage.

Abaddon sniggered. "Is that the best you've got?" he asked. "I thought you were cleverer."

"I don't have time for a war of words with you."

"It seems to me you have all the time in the world. It's not like you're doing much in the way of actually fighting me," the Destroyer said. "Perhaps words were all you ever really had."

"I told you before that you won't win."

"I remember. But I don't think you believe it now." The Beast kicked Lucas's body with his heavy foot. "Now you see that I was right, you're finally counting the cost and it's not adding up. No one will blame you for quitting."

Zoe wiped her stinging eyes. "I'm not quitting."

Abaddon walked over to Zoe and leaned in close to her ear. "Haven't you already?" he asked.

Zoe jerked her head toward his sneering face and then back to Lucas's pale form. Beside it appeared the lifeless bodies of the others stacked together in a bloody heap at her feet.

Abaddon leaned back in. "You can't withstand this...you can't withstand me."

* * *

Zoe sat up with a gasp. Her mouth still tasted like metal, and smoke scorched her nostrils. She wiped her wet cheeks with the sleeve of her sweater and stood up, pulling her blanket tight around her to ward off the chill, and then headed downstairs to get a drink. The house was quiet except for the creak of the wooden steps under her feet and the quiet mumbling coming from the living room. Zoe changed direction to peek in.

The fireplace held only a few glowing embers to warm and light the dark space. Another murmur drew her eyes from the fireplace to the figure on the couch. Alex flipped over, tossing his blanket onto the floor as he groaned. Zoe sighed, picked up the flannel throw from the floor, and gently re-covered Alex. She tossed another log into the fireplace and stooped down to stoke the embers until a flame sprung to life. She watched it for a moment, letting its warmth wash over her.

Alex mumbled again. Zoe stood, observing him. She wondered briefly what he dreamed of, then shook off her concern as he became more peaceful. In Zoe's experience, the dreams that warranted concern—the ones that were really nightmarish attacks from their enemy— never ended peacefully, at least not on their own. *It's probably nothing worth noting.* Zoe continued on to the kitchen as the faint light of the sun began to peek up over the horizon.

CHAPTER FOUR

Claire sat on the front porch steps, sipping her customary steaming cup of coffee. Her cardigan was wrapped tight around her shoulders and her body hunched in for warmth amidst the dreary winter day.

Claire heard the familiar sound of flapping wings and felt a warm gust ruffle her hair. "Are you not cold out here?" Michael asked.

Claire took another long swallow from her mug. "I needed some fresh air," she said and patted the spot next to her on the stoop.

Michael sat, his hands clasped together and his posture straight "You did not get enough sleep."

She curled one lip up slyly and arched an eyebrow. "Are you saying I look tired?" she asked. "That I'm not my normal gorgeous self?"

"No...I did not mean..." The Guardian flinched.

Claire giggled softly. "Just giving you a hard time, big guy. A girl needs to grab a laugh where she can get one these days."

"And it is acceptable to laugh at my expense?"

Claire felt her mouth droop before she saw the glint of humor in Michael's illuminated eyes. She chuckled again, but it broke apart with an invasive thought that she had been unable to keep at bay. "It was my fault," she whispered, the weight of her conviction, always looming, threatening to crush every moment of peace and joy.

"It was not," the angel replied.

She felt the pain and guilt squeeze together inside her chest and strangle her heart. "I let her go. After all she'd done, I had her in my hands and I let her go."

"It was to save a life. It was worth it. Charlie was worth it." Michael laid his hand gently on her knee.

"Losing Lucas wasn't. I hesitated and it opened the door...I..." Her strength began to waver and the memory of what had happened echoed in the tremble of her voice.

Michael took the cup from her and set it down on the porch. She felt one of his hands touch the small of her knee while his other pulled her chin toward him. His voice was stern as he said, "Lucas made a choice, a selfless one. Don't take that away from him by feeling guilty that it wasn't you."

Claire took a deep, cleansing breath. She tucked herself into Michael's arms, leaning her head against his chest. "It shouldn't have been anyone."

"No, it should not," he replied. "But war always brings death." He leaned his cheek against the top of her head. "And war does not stop when death comes."

Another gulp of air filled Claire's lungs and she exhaled a foggy puff. "Our grief must wait."

"No, it will not wait. But we must not let it stop us."

* * *

Alex's warm breath frosted the glass on the front door, but it was coldness that filled his veins and pumped through his heart, darkness washing over his spying eyes. *She would still love me if...*

He tried to shake off the dangerous, jealous thoughts. He felt the chilly signs of his undoing retreat from the surface of his skin into the depths of his waning soul. He wanted to be stronger, but he knew he was slipping away from himself. He sensed the pulling and the tugging of the darkness on his mind, body, and soul. He could feel his resolve weakening, and it was becoming harder to fight. The darkness seemed to always be there, just lying in wait for his final relinquishing.

CHAPTER FIVE

The donut box came sliding across the counter at Zoe.

"You should eat something," Daniel said.

She flipped the lid open and stared at the half-dozen pastries left inside. She wanted to refuse them but the growl in her stomach wouldn't let her, so she pulled out a glazed donut and took a tiny bite.

"Thank you." Daniel smiled and handed her a napkin. "Have you talked to Maggie?"

"Some," Zoe replied. "I think she's coming over later." She took a larger bite, filling her mouth as the hunger she had abated took charge.

"How is she?" Daniel bit into his bear claw.

Zoe shook her heavy head. "She's Maggie. Looking on the bright side is her super power." Zoe was sure her words sounded meaner than she meant them to. She wanted to be glad that her friend wasn't drowning like she was, but it made her angry. In some way, they all made her angry. They were moving back into the routines of real life: eating, working, talking, sleeping. With each minute that passed, they were taking another step away from Lucas while she wasn't ready to leave him behind. It had been the same when her parents had died. How had she gotten past that? How had she started living again then? She couldn't remember now. That was another lifetime ago. That was when she was just a girl taking ballet and going to high school. That was when she was normal. She wasn't that girl anymore. She was the Daughter. She was chosen. And she was going to lose them all before it was over.

Daniel interrupted her thoughts.

"And you?" he asked with quiet hesitation. "Are you okay?"

"Am I supposed to be?" She dropped her donut back in the box and shoved it away.

"Zoe, I didn't mean...I'm just asking...I'm worried about you."

"I know, Daniel. I'm sorry."

When Daniel scooted his chair closer, Zoe expected a lecture was coming her way. Instead, he touched her face, the rough callouses on his hand comforting against her cheek. "Don't be sorry. You have every right to be angry, to be sad. But, you need to talk about it. Keeping it all inside is just going to drive you down a path you don't want to be on. Trust me, I know."

Zoe's lips quivered and she pulled them tight, not letting herself cry again. "I'm afraid."

"Of what?" Daniel asked.

"That Lucas won't be the last one I lose." Speaking the words cracked the inner wall she had been building and tears spilled over it.

Daniel wrapped his hand around to the back of her head and pulled her close.

Zoe melted into him, allowing herself a moment of weakness, a moment of comfort even if it felt superficial, only temporarily appeasing the ache. She could feel the pain rebuilding its walls even as Daniel whispered soft words to her. She longed for them to be enough but knew they didn't hold that much power. No matter how much she wished they could, words were never going to be enough to make this right.

CHAPTER SIX

Claire walked into Charlie's hospital room.

Garrett was sitting in the corner chair, EM's journal open on his lap. "I thought Alex was coming with you?" he asked.

"He said he needed to run some errands, get some air. He'll meet me here in a little while."

Garrett nodded and then returned to the scribbled words on the wrinkled pages. "How could Mom and Dad keep us from the others?"

Claire squatted on the arm of his chair and read over her brother's shoulder. "I don't know. Even if they wanted to protect the Chronicle and the map, they didn't have to isolate themselves from the whole community. Retreating from everything and everyone was the wrong move. They may have protected the key but they didn't protect us."

Garrett closed the book. "All those years we could have had people helping us. We could have more help now."

"I know." Claire stood back up and stepped closer to Charlie's bed. "He came," she said, staring down at her comatose friend, "and he said more would come before it was over."

"Will they be enough?" Garret asked.

She squeezed the old man's hand. "I hope so."

Garrett stood and gazed out of the window, the warm colors of the sunset casting a subtle glow across his face. "Maybe we can hedge our bets."

"What do you mean?" Claire kept hold of Charlie's hand as a twinge of fear fluttered down her spine.

"I talked to Michael," her brother answered. "He thinks more guardians will come fight with the Daughter and the Armor-Bearer."

"And we get them to join us how?"

"We get them a message. Let them know what's happening, that it's time." Garrett continued to look out the window. Claire could see the vibrant sunset beyond her brother's silhouette; its pink and orange hues were painted across the dimming sky.

"So we have not because we've asked not?" she questioned.

"Basically."

Claire moved beside Garrett, her shoulder brushing against his arm. "But they only take orders from the Maker. Does Michael really need to go back just to ask for help? Can't we just..."

"The Maker is the one who told him to take a message to the others."

"So he left?" The question squeaked out painfully.

"No." Garrett ran a shaky hand through his hair before looking her in the eye. "And he isn't going to be leaving. I am."

She choked on his words. "What? No, Garrett, you just got back. You can't—Zoe won't be able to handle losing you again."

Garrett pulled her into his chest. "It's okay, bird," he whispered. "Michael brought me back so you and I could make things right, so that you and Zoe wouldn't have anything to hold you back from doing what needs to be done. You will both be okay. After all, you need him more than you need me."

* * *

"No! You can't leave me again!" Zoe shook in her father's arms.

"We were so lucky to get to see each other again," her father said. "Do you know how many people wish for this kind of chance?"

"I don't care, Dad. I don't want you to go." She sobbed into his chest.

"It's for the best, Zo. I was never really meant to come back. The Maker allowed it, but it was never going to be forever. Besides, I'm sure your mom is wondering where I've been. She will be so proud of you."

Zoe could feel her father's tears wetting her hair.

"I have to go," he muttered against the top of her head.

Zoe pulled away from him and wiped her face with her sleeve.

"I love you." The kiss her father planted on her forehead was warm, but not as comforting as Zoe remembered from childhood.

"I love you too." Her voice cracked in sync with her heart.

Zoe sunk into another embrace from her father, possibly the last one she would ever experience. She snuggled against him, listening to his heartbeat, feeling his chest move with each breath. She inhaled the musky scent of his aftershave. She didn't want to let go.

"Take care of her," he whispered to someone over her shoulder.

"I will," Claire replied.

"It is time," Michael said, placing a hand on Garrett's shoulder.

Garrett let go of Zoe. She didn't protest further though every fiber of her being wanted to. Her father reached to brush away the tears she could feel hanging under her lashes. A wide smile spread under his own glassy eyes as he said, "Always remember, you are powerful, you are chosen, you are loved, and you are never alone."

With the flap of wings and a warm breeze, he was gone.

Her father's embrace disappeared, but a new set of arms wrapped around Zoe—Claire, helping hold her together.

CHAPTER SEVEN

"Knock-knock," Maggie called, popping her head in the doorway of Zoe's room. "Can I come in?"

"Since when do you ask?" Zoe cocked a brow. Maggie noticed her eyes were red and glazed and could tell Zo had been crying.

"Since my best friend has decided she wants to be alone all the time."

"Sorry, Mags." Zoe was curled up in a blanket, leaning against her headboard with her knees pulled tight against her chest.

Maggie hopped onto the bed and replied, "It's not okay."

"Excuse me?" Zoe asked.

"We've all lost people. We all lost Lucas. You can't keep acting like you're the only one who feels it."

For a moment, Zoe's mouth resembled a fish's, just opening and closing over and over like she was gulping imaginary water. Finally she responded, "I'm the only one who's responsible."

"Says who? Abaddon?" Maggie asked and crossed her arms over her chest. "You know better than that."

"Just because he lies doesn't mean he's lying about this," Zoe said. "Helping me is only going to get you all killed."

Maggie scooted closer to Zoe and tucked her own knees up

matching her friend's posture. She considered her words before responding. "One—you can't know that for sure. And two—it's not up to you to decide for *us* what *we* are willing to do."

"You want to die?" Zoe questioned.

"No, I don't *want* to die, but that doesn't mean I'm not willing to put myself in that realm of possibility for my friends, my family," Maggie replied. "You may be the Daughter, but you're not the only one who is chosen. We all can play a part in stopping the Destroyer and saving the world. You don't get to decide that, and you aren't responsible for us, Zoe."

"I feel like I am."

"Because you've been listening to the wrong voice." Maggie put her arm around Zoe's shoulder and pulled her friend to lean against her. "Once upon a time, someone told me I was becoming a dietary supplement. That a thing was feeding off my grief and pain, and we came up with this awesome plan to stop it by not giving it anything to eat."

"And that worked?" Zoe asked.

Maggie chuckled. "Yeah, it actually did. It still does."

"I think you're stronger than me, Mags."

"Nah, we're just stronger together."

Silence filled the space between them for a brief moment before Zoe's voice shattered it.

"My dad is gone," Zoe said.

"Claire told me."

"I know I shouldn't be sad but—"

"No one said you shouldn't be sad," Maggie interrupted. "Just don't be consumed by it, or alone with it."

"Daniel told me the same thing."

"Sometimes he's smart." Maggie chuckled.

"I'm glad you're here, Mags."

"Of course you are. I light up your life with happiness."

Zoe's giggle faded into a deep sigh and she said, "I'm sorry I haven't been there for you, Maggie. I know how you felt about Lucas, how you were starting to feel anyway."

A lump formed in the back of Maggie's throat. "It comes in waves. I think I'm okay and then something reminds me of him, what he would say, what he would do, that stupid smirk."

"You loved that smirk."

"Yeah, I did."

"It wasn't worth it." Zoe said as she leaned against her friend. "None of this feels worth it, ya know?"

Maggie concentrated on her fingers fidgeting with the blanket, afraid to look up, to look at Zoe as she tried to make sense of her own thoughts, her own grief, and her own pain. Things like this never really made sense though; they couldn't. She wanted it to make sense. She wanted to see the big picture, know all the reasons, have all the explanations. Even if she had them, it wouldn't take away the pain because he would still be gone. But there were always slivers of hope, pieces you could hold on to—to pull you out of the pit. She needed to find one of those pieces now. She needed to hold tight to it. She was sure Zoe needed it too.

Maggie took her friend's hand. "The world will never feel like it's worth more than the one person you love. Losing Lucas will never feel worth it to us, but I bet it felt worth it to him. He died for the people he loved. That's the tragic beauty of it."

CHAPTER EIGHT

The map was rolled out on the kitchen table, its tattered edges curling upward. Claire smoothed a particularly unruly corner down and then held it in place with an empty juice glass.

"Refill?" Alex asked, handing her a full mug of black coffee.

"No cream?"

"Sorry, chief. We're all out."

Claire took a sip and said, "I guess the groceries aren't going to buy themselves."

"I'll run by the store after checking in on Charlie. Daniel could probably use a tap out right about now anyway."

"Thank you." Claire smiled, returning her attention to scribbles arranged outside the boundaries of an ancient topography. Alex's soft lips caressed her cheek.

"I'll be back in a couple of hours," he said.

"Be careful...and don't forget the cream."

"Have you made any progress?" Michael's deep voice interrupted the clicking of the door and Alex's goodbye.

"Some," Claire answered. "The code being in Hebrew has made for slow going. If only the map translated itself like the Chronicle, my life would be easy."

"I can help with that. Hebrew is a language I am familiar with." Claire moved over giving Michael room to see the symbols written on the cracked parchment. "Knock yourself out," she said.

Michael raised an eyebrow which elicited a giggle from Claire. She sipped her coffee while the Guardian began to write his translations.

It didn't take long for Michael to fill several notebook pages with numbers he had translated from the map. Claire was right beside him with the Chronicle open in front of her, ready to begin the work of deciphering the ancient message when she heard chatter on the stairs.

"If you're looking for food, you're going to have to order something because, well, life," Claire called over her shoulder.

"Your mom game is *so* on point lately," Zoe said, giving Claire a patronizing pat on the shoulder as she passed by on her way into the kitchen.

"Someone is getting her sass back. I like it." Claire raised an eyebrow. "I think."

"Food?" Maggie asked, resting her elbows on the table and leaning against them so her bright smile protruded into Claire's view.

"Chinese would be nice," Claire replied. "Money is in my purse. And get extra egg rolls because Alex always eats mine."

"Do we have a takeout menu in here?" Zoe asked, rummaging through a kitchen drawer. "Where is Alex anyway?"

Claire checked her watch, her nose wrinkling up when she saw the time. "He was supposed to be giving Daniel a break at the hospital and then getting groceries."

"I'm guessing your confused expression means you're wondering why Daniel hasn't shown up here yet?" Zoe flipped the menu over and pulled her phone from her back pocket.

Claire made eye contact with Michael who had stopped

working on his translation. "Perhaps he went back to the barn for some rest," he said.

"I'll call him after I order to find out," Zoe offered. "He isn't going to want to miss food."

The sound of flipping pages caught Claire's attention. Maggie had picked up the Chronicle and was looking between it and the map as she asked, "So if Hebrew is read right to left, do we cipher the text that way? Or left to right because the Chronicle translates itself into English?"

Claire ran her hand through her hair and then arched her back to stretch her tired muscles. "I've been asking myself that same question." She picked her pen back up. "I guess we do both and see what makes sense, but Hebrew would be where I would start since that's the original language."

"But the coding on the map seems to be scribbled all over the place without rhyme or reason so how do we even know we're starting in the right place there?" Zoe asked, rejoining the conversation after having placed their dinner order.

"Welcome to my headache." Claire tossed her pen back down. "There has to be something we're missing. We can't just run the code in every possible order and variation. We don't have that kind of time."

Michael paused in his work, sitting up straighter. "The veil grows weaker by the day," he said. More shadows are tearing through and feeding Abaddon's strength. No, we do not have time for guessing."

"Guessing what?" asked Daniel. Claire looked up to see him shrugging off his coat as he came in the kitchen. "I hope it's something to do with dinner."

"We were just wondering where you were," said Zoe, walking around the table to kiss his cheek. "And dinner is on the way."

"You're in a good mood," he said. "I came straight here as soon as Alex took my spot sitting with Charlie."

Claire's wrinkled her brow. "He just got there? He left here over an hour ago."

Daniel shrugged. "Maybe he ran some errands or something. I don't know."

"Lucas would be crossing his arms and telling us something hinky was going on," Maggie said, her lips curled downward, her eyes dimming just a little.

The air seemed to thicken at the mention of his name. Claire smiled at the thought of Lucas leaning against the kitchen counter with a mischievous grin, another snarky comment undoubtedly waiting on the tip of his tongue.

"That he would," Claire said. "But all things hinky will have to wait. This map is priority." She took a deep breath and pulled her hair up into a messy bun to get it out of her face while she worked.

Claire could feel someone breathing across the back of her neck. "It's weird, it looks kind of like your scar," she heard Maggie say directly over her shoulder.

"What?" Claire jerked around to address Maggie who was squinting at the map. She pushed her chair back so she could stand and get a better look. Michael, Daniel, and Zoe all gathered in close around her.

"See, here…" Maggie forced her way to the front of the tight huddle and pointed her finger along the left side of the handwriting. "If you imagine that the scribbles were a big, solid line and extended over the map part instead of just around it, then they curve around like the lettering of your brand."

"She is correct," said Michael as he traced along each line of Hebrew with his finger like he was writing each letter in his mind. Then he went back to his beginning at the top corner and pointed at the letter on the far right. "That would mean we start here."

CHAPTER NINE

Alex, following the pull of the demons that now inhabited his mind, slid the large steel warehouse door open. He saw Meredith jump from her chair, knife in hand, ready to defend their makeshift home. She was subdued by the twitch of the Destroyer's fingers.

Abaddon calmly placed the book he was holding down on his side table. "I hadn't been expecting any visitors but I guess it was only a matter of time before you—"

"What did you do to me?" Alex's voice bounced off the warehouse walls, his angry breath puffing like smoke in front of him.

"I helped you, remember?" Abaddon said, relaxing back into his chair with the leisure of a king on his throne.

"I didn't want any part of this but I can feel it—you—itching under my skin, inside my mind all the time. I told you no, that I wouldn't help you. "

"Your mouth said no, Alex, but your heart said yes. Blackened little thing that it has become." The Destroyer smirked as he spoke. "It didn't take much to shrivel it, mold it to my whim. Envy and anger are quick workers."

"You... you've been pulling my strings since before you even brought me back? All of this has been some game to you." Alex surged forward but was halted by the sharp steel of Meredith's blade against his ribcage.

Abaddon had gotten up from his chair and was moving toward Alex, his black eyes blazing. "None of this is a game, boy. This is survival. This is victory over my enemy. This is everything I have spent centuries working for coming to pass." Alex watched as the calloused flesh of a human hand dissolved into molten rock tipped by obsidian claws right before it gripped his throat. The Destroyer's breath bit Alex's skin. He saw volcanic fangs take the place of Abaddon's previous pearly smile. "You would do well to accept the gift I have given you. I grow tired of your sniveling."

Alex fought for the air to speak. "I love her and she will never be able to love me again if I become what you're asking."

Meredith's seductive whisper tickled the back of his neck. "Poor dear, Claire never loved you. It was the idea of you, of a happily ever after. She didn't mourn you—she mourned her dreams of escape. I saw it in her nightmares. You were just a means to an end for her." The pinch of her blade released, and delicate fingers danced up his arm until her hand came to rest on his shoulder. "But it's her loss. You deserved better than what *she* offered you."

Icy darkness moved through Alex's veins as it came out of hiding, creeping along the lines under his skin and flooding all the parts he had kept it from until no corner of him was left free from its grasp. He sucked in the musty air of the warehouse as the crushing on his windpipe subsided. Abaddon had let go and was stepping backward with a satisfied smirk as Alex exhaled a long, icy breath.

Meredith stepped in front of him, tucking her dagger back into its keeping. Her hands come to rest against his chest. "Do you feel it? The power he's given you?"

Alex's dipped his head in a curt nod.

"You can have anything you want—*take* what you want." He peered into Meredith's black eyes, watched the flutter of her long lashes as her tongue grazed her bottom lip. "What do you want, Alex?"

"I want what was taken from me," he replied. "The life I should have had—that I deserved."

"Then you shall have it," Abaddon said, sliding back into his chair. "I reward those who serve me."

CHAPTER TEN

"Thanks for the cream," Claire said, pausing in her work to watch Alex trudge into the kitchen, rubbing his fingers through his messy hair.

"No problem." He yawned and poured himself a cup of coffee with barely a glance at Claire.

It wasn't like him. He had come in late while she, Michael, and the girls had been working on the translation. He'd put away the groceries with no more than a nod and a grunt. He'd glanced at their progress and then gone to bed. And now he hardly acknowledged her, no customary kiss on the cheek, no warm smile.

"Everything okay?" she asked.

"Yeah, just tired I guess." He took a sip of his black coffee. "Maybe I'm coming down with something."

Claire stood and walked over to Alex. She reached out to touch his face and he retreated from it.

"If I am sick, the last thing we need is for you to catch it," he said.

Claire swallowed softly and then bit her bottom lip. "You've been doing so much to keep all of us going the past few days. I know I've been distracted and I'm sorry, but if there is something I can do for you, just ask."

Alex touched her arm gently. "No, I'm fine. It's probably nothing that a little more rest won't cure."

Claire nodded and watched him walk back into the living room. A chill ran across her arms. She pulled her sweater tighter and forced her worries to a distance.

"No breakfast?" Maggie's voice broke Claire's introspection.

"She's too busy to cook for the mere mortals," Zoe added, following Maggie into the kitchen.

"Can't the mere mortals cook for themselves?" Claire asked as she turned and leaned against the counter.

Maggie pulled the juice from the refrigerator. "They can, but last time they tried, they nearly caught the kitchen on fire."

"Ah, yes, the great muffin incident of 2016. 'Twas a dark day," Zoe said, laying her head on Claire's shoulder.

"If I remember correctly, didn't someone manage to make me pancakes for my birthday?" Claire asked.

"Trade secret—they were frozen. She gave you the illusion of homemade pancakes for your birthday," Maggie said in a whisper as if this wasn't something she should reveal, and Zoe wasn't standing right there.

Zoe pouted her lip and batted her eyelashes. "It's the thought that counts, right?"

Claire rolled her eyes and sighed. "If I'm going to make pity eggs, you might as well call Daniel to come over. A boy can't live by cereal alone."

"I'll text him," Zoe said already typing on her phone. "Thanks heaps. You're the best." She kissed Claire's cheek.

"Let's not forget that," Claire said.

"Never." The girls responded in unison.

"So are we any closer to finishing this bad boy and grabbing me a mystical sword?" Zoe asked while flipping through the legal pad that sat on the dining table.

Claire pulled out her skillet. "A little. Michael and I worked another hour after you two went to sleep, and then I crashed. I'm thinking directions to said mystical sword will be finished today or tomorrow."

A stool scratched against the wood floors as Maggie pulled it out and then plopped onto it. She leaned forward and rested her chin in her hands, a cheeky grin across her face. "Speaking of Michael, where's Alex?"

"Resting. He said he isn't feeling well," Claire replied.

There was a sudden quiet in the kitchen as Zoe stopped her page turning. "You say that like you don't believe him," she said.

Claire paused briefly before cracking another egg into a glass bowl. "I say it like I'm worried about him. A lot has been thrown on him. Trying to keep up with all of us can be stressful."

"Not to mention being jealous of a frickin' angel," Maggie chimed in. "I mean, talk about competition."

Claire glared at her over her scrambling. "No one is competing for anything."

"You keep telling yourself that," Maggie said with a wink.

Zoe chuckled as she wrapped her arm around Claire's shoulder. "I mean, we know humans and guardians aren't supposed to mix. And Michael knows that. But, does Alex? Do you? Cuz you and Michael have history. You're close—no matter how you spin it in your head."

"Nothing will happen between me and Michael," Claire said. She was becoming slightly annoyed by the girls' interrogation.

"Are you sure? Because I think your half-angel babies would be the most adorable little abominations." Maggie sat up straighter, her eyes squinting a little as she asked, "What if he became human?"

Claire stopped stirring. "Have I time warped because I feel like I have had this conversation before. Angels don't just become human."

"But if they did?" Maggie asked.

"They don't," Claire replied.

"But—" Zoe began.

Claire huffed. "Look, I know you two find some sort of sick enjoyment perpetuating this little love triangle fantasy you've concocted, but guardians don't become human, humans and guardians don't fall in love, and my feelings for Alex have nothing to do with Michael."

"So you still have feelings for Alex?" Maggie asked, leaning in a little closer again, her small smirk returning.

Claire dropped her whisk and her head. "You're exasperating."

"It's her gift." Zoe giggled. "And for the record, we haven't concocted anything. We are just reading the field, and whatever the rules are, there are two guys who both have feelings for you, and at least one of them is getting jealous over the other, Aunt Claire. So you might want to clarify said rules to him and decide exactly what you do and don't feel."

Claire's pursed lips loosened. She opened her mouth but closed it again, taking in what her niece was saying. Had she really been so oblivious? Had she bottled up her feelings for Michael for so long that she didn't see them spilling out now? Why couldn't she stop them? She knew she shouldn't feel these things. She knew that they had to fight any temptations to be more to each other. But it wasn't so easy. They were connected. That's all this was. It wasn't love or attraction. It was the tethering of their souls creating a bond that merely mimicked those emotions. Wasn't it? Did Alex have something to be jealous over? Did she even still love him? She had loved Alex once, of that she was sure. She had been ready to spend the rest of her life with him, and then he had died, and she'd mourned him to the point that it had almost killed her. But now, did she still love him? Was he still the man she wanted to spend her forever with? Or was that the fantasy? A happily-ever-after life with a normal picket fence and a normal job and a normal guy?

Claire shifted her focus back to mixing the bowl of yolks. "I don't like it when you're so insightful and mature," she said.

Zoe sighed dramatically. "Me neither."

CHAPTER ELEVEN

Zoe slid out of the truck behind Daniel. As she shut the door she said, "Are you sure you're ready for this?" She was watching Maggie who had zipped up her jacket and was now fixing a small arrow into the crossbow Charlie had given her.

"Not even a little bit, but I'm going to do it anyway because I want to help," Mags replied.

Zoe checked the knives she had tucked in her wool coat and secured her lion dagger in her boot. "There are other ways you can help besides patrolling with us, Mags," she said.

"I refuse to merely be comic relief. I also refuse to sit at home with Claire taking notes and being mopey," Maggie answered.

"Why is she mopey again?" Daniel asked as he came from around the back of the truck to join them.

"Trying to make tough life choices, cliché love triangles, and a general lack of fun in her life," Maggie said with an exaggerated shoulder shrug and a chuckle.

"Oh yeah, she needs a hobby. Let's sign her up for a book club, or Zumba class," Zoe interjected in a snide tone.

Maggie shook her head. "Your sarcasm is uncalled for, Zoe Renee," she said.

Zoe felt Daniel's warm breath on her ear as he whispered in mock fear, "Did she just use your middle name?"

"I feel a Gilmore Girls reference coming on, which will only serve to perpetuate this conversation, so I'm going to refrain from using it and say we get started so we can get this over with and get back home," Zoe replied. She adjusted her knit hat, pulling it down to guard her ears from the winter chill. "Let's go."

Daniel grabbed her arm gently. "Hey, are you sure *you're* ready for this?" he asked.

"I'm fine," Zoe answered. "I just want us to be extra careful with Maggie out here for the first time."

"And you think we wouldn't be, Zo?" His forehead wrinkled above his worried eyes.

"No, I just...Let's just be on guard."

"Hey, I wouldn't have come if I didn't think I could handle it." Maggie was holding up her miniature bow, waving it a little. "Plus I've been practicing," she said.

"And you can actually hit the target?" Daniel asked with raised eyebrows.

"More often than before," Maggie responded.

"I guess that's something," Daniel said with a smile.

"I'll stay at a safe distance and scream bloody murder if anything comes close to me and then huddle in the fetal position like a big rock so you can swoop in and kill it." Maggie said, drawing an X across her chest with her index finger.

"Promise?" Zoe forced a more casual expression, trying to pinch her cheeks into some half-hearted smile.

"I crossed my heart didn't I?"

"She did," Daniel said. "And you're totally going to make this rock formation thing a thing now aren't you?" he asked Maggie.

"You know it," she replied with a wink.

"Let's just get going, please," Zoe finally conceded. She turned and started the trek down the sidewalk toward the park.

Things seemed strange at night. During the daylight hours, even in winter, there was always some activity here. Joggers would be pounding the pavement of the small track that circled the perimeter. People walked their dogs. Children played on the colorful playground. Under this blanket of darkness, it was much more eerie. The wind rustled through dead branches, replacing the summer song of tree frogs and crickets, and the rays of the moon created shadows of each limb as cracked lines along the ground. In the daytime, this place was nothing but life, but in the dark of December, it seemed like only death.

Zoe clenched her fists and squared her shoulders. The smoldering battleground of her nightmares flashed like a slideshow through her mind. The shadowy grass of the park was a reminder of that horrid landscape she couldn't shake free from. She bit the inside of her cheek, trying to regain her grip on reality.

"Is it windy enough for that to be happening?" Maggie asked, pointing toward a red and blue seesaw that was beginning to teeter back and forth, its hinges squeaking with the movement.

"No, it isn't," Daniel answered, a knife already in his hand.

The low whistle of a slowly turning merry-go-round and the creaking movement of the swing set created a creepy chorus that filled the silent night. The melody of customary hissing joined the arrangement, swirling in on an icy wind that drew goosebumps up Zoe's arms and down her spine. She squatted to retrieve her dagger from its keep, rising with it gripped tightly, ready as the demons glared from their perches all over the small playground.

Zoe felt Maggie's arm brush hers as Maggie leaned close to ask, "When would be a good time to shoot one?"

"I'd prefer that you go right to rock formation," Zoe replied, but her eyes never left the ensemble that was now drooling ash from its many barred fangs. "Daniel, you take the swings on the left. I'll take everything to the right. Maggie stay back and shoot anything that looks at you," she ordered, then took the first step toward the seesaw. She paused to give one last glance over her shoulder. "Oh, and Mags," she called, "don't miss."

To her relief, Maggie lifted her bow with steady hands. "Yeah. Got it chief."

Zoe gave a nod to Daniel and the two charged at the shadows before them. Sulfur stung Zoe's cold nose. The rustling of chains at the swing set and shrill shrieks signaled each demon's demise. But Zoe didn't dare turn to verify Daniel's triumphs. She was focused on her own task. There were at least five shadows that she could see, and she was sure more had to be waiting in the darkness of nearby branches. "Maggie keep your eyes open!" she yelled.

"I'd be too afraid to close them!" came Maggie's comforting response.

Zoe lunged at the first two shadows that had perched themselves on the teeter-totter. She stabbed her dagger into the first while drawing one of Lucas's throwing knives and flinging it at the other. As they dissolved, she turned toward the three that had dug their claws into the old wooden merry-go-round. She ran and leaped onto the turning wheel, tossing another knife into one's forehead, and then thrust her lion blade into a second. The third reached out, planting its nails in her shoulder. She could feel the burn through her jacket but bit back the pain with a low growl. She spun around and drove her dagger into its hollow chest.

"Zoe!" Maggie cried out the warning just before the shadow in front of Zoe turned to ash and another jumped onto her back.

Zoe was pushed forward and fell onto the wood beneath her. She kicked and squirmed until she was able to roll. She shoved the demon off of her and onto the ground just as an arrow struck its abdomen. But her relief was short lived as another shadow dropped from a high branch and landed on top of her, pinning her shoulders down. The force of it knocked the dagger out of her hand. She strained her fingers but couldn't quite reach it, so she grabbed the demon's wrists and pulled instead. She tore its grip loose from her shoulders and bucked up her hips so she could force it to roll off of her. Then Zoe made the switch, maneuvering herself so that she was now straddling the creature. She gripped its neck with her bare hands and it writhed underneath her, scratching at her arms and legs at it tried to break free.

"Zoe!" Daniel yelled.

"Zoe, stop!" Maggie screamed.

Zoe felt pain seer through the skin of her hands where they choked the demon under her. Blood was trickling down her arms and soaking into her sleeves. She could feel the cotton material clinging to her and only then realized there was no power flowing along with the blood in her veins. There was no light nor warmth emanating from her to kill the unholy vermin that was still struggling against her. Zoe's brows pinched together and she quickly searched for her dagger. She reached one hand to grab it, wincing when her tender skin gripped its handle. Her muscles quivered as she plunged the blade into the shadow with a frustrated roar. She stabbed it again and again and again, oblivious to the fact that her knife was only hitting ash and wood, until Daniel stopped her hand.

"Zo!" Daniel yelled again.

"Maggie?" Zoe's heart picked up its panicked pace as fear flooded it.

"I'm fine." Maggie replied. Zoe looked to see her standing next to the merry-go-round as it finally slowed to a complete stop.

"We need to get you home," Daniel said, gently taking Zoe's arm and helping her stand.

She felt her knees buckle as soon as she tried to take her own weight. Daniel caught her around her waist to keep her upright. He tossed Maggie the keys.

"You drive," he said as he scooped Zoe up into his arms.

Zoe silently stared at the blistering skin on the palms of her bloody hands as Daniel carried her to the car.

* * *

Zoe felt sick jostling in Daniel's arms as he burst through the front door yelling, "Claire! Michael!"

She saw a blurry Claire rush in from the kitchen. "What happened?"

"Is Michael here?" Daniel asked, setting Zoe down on the sofa.

41

The heavy steps of the Guardian echoed from the little hallway. "I am," he said.

"She needs your help." Zoe felt Daniel's clammy hand on hers, gingerly picking it up and turning it over to reveal her burns.

"I'm still waiting for the 'what happened' part," Claire said as Zoe let her aunt help her remove her coat.

"There were demons in the park," Maggie offered.

Zoe winced as Claire tried to peel back the fabric of her thermal Henley from the wet wounds under her sleeve. "Yeah, I figured demons were involved. But how did all this happen? How many were there? Where were the two of you?"

Daniel paced back and forth. He ran his hands through his hair, mussing it as he replied, "There were only ten, maybe twelve. I took half and Zoe took the other while Maggie—"

"While Maggie stood watch and shot one, thank you very much," Maggie said, finishing his sentence.

Daniel huffed. "Applause for you shooting one will have to wait a minute, Mags. Long story short—one got the jump on Zoe, and when I turned around from taking out my last shadow, she had flipped it and pinned it down with her bare hands."

Claire stroked Zoe's cheek, drawing her attention from Daniel. She gazed at her aunt, who tucked a strand of hair behind her ear and asked, "Zo, what were you thinking?"

"There's more to it," Daniel said. Zoe saw the worry etched around his eyes as he squatted in front of her. "You weren't yourself out there tonight...you were—"

"Vengeancy. She was all vengeancy," Maggie filled in, and then plopped down in her favorite corner spot.

Zoe rolled her eyes. "That isn't a real word."

"Perhaps not," Mags replied, "but it is the perfect adjective to describe you getting all stabby."

"Also not a word," Zoe said with a sigh.

Maggie opened her mouth, looking as if she had another retort ready, but Claire stopped her. "All right girls," she said, "enough sass. Real words or not, that doesn't sound like you, Zo."

Zoe grumbled to herself and sat back, only to lurch forward again as her back scraped against the couch, reminding her of the burn on her shoulder. She moved to touch it but stopped before inflicting more pain on her wounded hands. She shuddered at the sight of them and then turned back toward Claire's concerned glare. "I've done it before...the light...it didn't..." Tears slipped out suddenly, dripping quickly from her chin and stinging her skin.

"Let's take care of those first." Michael sat down next to Zoe and carefully placed his hands on her. His veins began to glow blue and his eyes grew brighter.

Zoe watched his eyes illuminate brilliantly as he stared at her wounds with intensity. Then she watched the blue light dance out from under the folded cuff of his rolled flannel and along the veins of his forearms and fingers. She felt it flow into her. It was like warm water, no...oil, was being poured over her palms, and then it glided up her arms until it reached the wound on her shoulder. It stretched down her stomach and legs, hitting every place of pain, at least on the surface. But there was a deeper pain that couldn't be impacted by the heat of Michael's healing touch. There was a fear that had taken hold inside of her. She could sense it rooting into her mind, digging farther down in the hopes of reaching her soul. Maybe it already had because she couldn't seem to fight it, couldn't stop it. Even in moments of laughter and relief, it was there, stealing all semblances of peace and tearing away any threads of hope.

"There," Michael said, and the warmth of his touch vanished.

"Why don't you go get cleaned up, Zo?" Claire said.

Zoe nodded. She intended to move but couldn't. It was like she had forgotten how to stand, how to walk, how to breathe. Her chest began to rise and fall faster. "The light didn't..."

"It did not leave you, if that is what you are worried about," Michael said.

Zoe stared into the Guardian's eyes again. They had dimmed but were still a brighter blue than anything human could be. "I don't understand what is happening to me, what I'm supposed to do."

"Maybe that is the problem," the Guardian responded. "You are trying too hard to understand rather than simply having faith."

Zoe sighed heavily.

"It's annoying when he's all cryptic and spiritual isn't it?" Claire said, her mouth curving into a wry grin as she nudged the Guardian's knee with her own.

"But he's right?" Zoe asked, picking at the blood crusting on her sleeve.

Claire's smile faltered but her eyes remained warm and full of care. "Yes, he is, which is also annoying."

Zoe tried to join in her aunt's playful tenor, but the fear hovered over her. "It's hard not to want answers, not to analyze."

"It is. But faith isn't something I can teach you," Claire said. Her aunt's calm hands covered her nervous ones, stilling them. "And it isn't something I can have for you no matter how much I wish that I could."

Zoe stretched out her sore muscles a bit as she stood up. "It's a good thing I'm too tired for any more questions or talking right now."

"I think there is one question we still need to answer," said Maggie, arms crossed and a slight pout on her face.

"What is that?" Daniel asked, crossing his own arms in mimicry.

"Am I going to get a cool scar now that I've killed a demon?" she asked.

After a short stunned silence, laughter broke through.

Zoe's mood briefly lightened. "That is a question I am okay with answering," she said. "That, and have we figured out my sword situation yet?"

"Actually," Claire began, "we may need to find your passports."

* * *

"I'm guessing those demons weren't just having recess on the playground?" Alex asked as he followed Meredith into the warehouse.

Abaddon didn't look up from his book. "I just wanted one more test run before we let the Daughter near the weapon. We needed to be sure we were still in control."

"She killed the shadows. Rather viciously, I might add. Is that us being in control?" Alex asked.

Meredith leaned her chin against Alex's shoulder and smiled up at him. "You're cute when you act all new and confused," she purred.

Alex flinched when Abaddon's book slammed closed. "A few demons had to be sacrificed. They are nothing. She can kill all the little foot soldiers she wants. There will always be more. They weren't the point."

Alex furrowed his brow.

Meredith tapped his nose with the tip of her finger. "Little Zo-glow didn't light up like a Christmas tree. She tried, she thought she was, but she didn't. That was the point."

"So she's too weak to use the sword?" Alex asked.

"Precisely." Abaddon's eyes blinked to black. "She will retrieve it, and even if we can't take it from her, when the time comes, the only thing she will be able to do with it is open the gates so that my entire army can sweep into this world and destroy all the lovely things I loathe."

CHAPTER TWELVE

"That can't be right." Zoe rubbed a towel through her wet hair.

"We checked it four times." Claire said. Her finger kept tapping the same spot on the old map. "This is the place."

"The Persian Gulf?" Zoe sat down at the table. "It's a body of water. How are we supposed to get a heavenly weapon from the bottom of a body of water?"

"Scuba gear?" Daniel shrugged at her with a grin.

Zoe punched him gently in the arm. "You're not cute."

"Of course I am and you know it," Daniel said and winked.

"Cute or not, he's wrong" said Claire, flipping through their translations. "The coordinates are for smack in the middle of the Persian Gulf, but I have a feeling we won't be getting wet."

"Care to explain?" Zoe asked.

"There were some additional instructions besides just GPS directions," Claire answered.

"At the edge of the city of Ur is the path to the Garden of God," Michael read over Claire's shoulder. Zoe eyed the words on the yellow page that Claire had underlined in bold black ink.

A crinkling of plastic drew her attention to Maggie who was unwrapping *another* lollipop. She stuck it in her mouth and mumbled, "Can nothing be specific and helpful? Why all the cryptic? Why can't it just say, 'Take the third street on the left and go seven-point-two miles and your destination will be on your right'?"

"I'm guessing this is a one-step-at-a-time sort of mission, and step one is to get to the city of Ur," Zoe said as she clutched her towel tight between her fingers. This was it. This was the first step to the end. Her heart thumped harder, faster, and she tried to slow its rhythm. She wanted to have hope. She knew she should, but images of death and failure had killed it. She wore a practiced smile on the outside, telling herself that vulnerability and honesty served no purpose, because the others couldn't possibly understand. They hadn't seen what she had. They weren't the ones holding the weight of the world on their shoulders and crumbling beneath it. They would tell her it was fine, that she should trust, that they were brave enough, that faith was the answer, that she wasn't alone in this. They were wrong. Were they wrong? Maybe— maybe not. She didn't know anymore. She didn't know what she believed, or what she wanted, or if she could do this. She wished she could go back to that first glimpse of the truth, sitting on her bed, reading the Chronicle and talking to Claire. She wished she could tell her aunt no and take back the courageous and ignorant desire to fight. Could she? Could she just walk away now, give up and hand over this heavy mantle to someone else?

Zoe entertained that thought longer than she should have, silently watching her family talk about travel plans and what to pack. Her false smile didn't falter while the cracks in her heart grew deeper. She wanted to stand up and scream and let them know how broken she felt.

"You okay?" Claire touched her clenched hands.

Would everyone please stop asking me that?

"Yeah, just tired. If we are going to save the world, I'm going to need some sleep."

Claire stretched. "We all are," she said.

* * *

The familiar voice of Zoe's adversary followed a line of black smoke that slithered over the tarnished landscape. The Destroyer's slinking words wafted around her. "Time revolved in an eternal loop. The knowledge of all that had been and all that was to come danced together like the pure white flames of the blazing fire. No hand need touch the sword, no hammer to bend it into form. Divine thought forged this blade of a metal not known to man, glistening like gold and stronger than steel. Divinity's fire keeps it protected from those who are not worthy to wield it."

"Waxing poetic today?" Zoe said with a exaggerated yawn.

Abaddon grew into shape as he crossed the expanse of blood and ash and came close enough for her to feel his chill. He began circling her and whispered, "Don't you recognize the passage? Are you so unfamiliar with your little magical book?"

"It's from the Chronicle?" Was it? Zoe was unsure. It had the same cadence, but she couldn't remember ever reading those words.

"One would think you would have taken notes on the most important bits, including anything having to do with the Eden Sword. That is what the Guardian called it?"

He kept circling, the motion making her a little sick. "You know about the sword?" she asked.

"I know about a lot of things," he said. "I know about prophecies and maps and swords and weak little girls who will fail."

"I will not fail."

Abaddon roared with laughter. "You lie so well. I'm actually quite impressed."

"It's not a lie. I am stronger than you."

"Now you're just showing off," he taunted. "I mean, if I couldn't see into that little broken spirit of yours, I might believe you."

Zoe's pulse elevated as her blood coursed faster through her veins. Her head began to ache at the sensation, and Abaddon's voice was muffled by the pounding in her ears.

"Just go ahead and give up," the Destroyer hissed, "let someone else be the hero. Let someone else make the sacrifice. You were never cut out for this."

Zoe's growl turned into a roar and she threw out her hand, waiting for the light to sting the beast.

Abaddon smirked. "Well, well, well. Anger looks good on you. Too bad it isn't the righteous kind or this moment could have been much scarier for me. Maybe you don't have to quit. Maybe the Maker has given up on you. Go ahead and get your sword"— Abaddon morphed from his granite form into a snake of thick, black smog that constricted around her—"*if* you are still worthy of it."

* * *

The first hints of daylight shimmered beyond the pale curtains as Zoe awoke. She felt a weight squeezing her lungs and sat up clutching her chest. When she was finally able to catch her breath, acute nausea rushed in with it. Zoe ran to the bathroom, crashing onto the floor in front of the toilet to vomit up the fear and agony. Even when there was nothing left in her stomach, those two relentless emotions continued to strangle her soul. She slid down, curling into a ball on the cool tile floor, crying, aching for relief from this pain.

"Have you forgotten me?" Zoe whispered.

There was only the cold floor and silence.

CHAPTER THIRTEEN

Claire watched as Alex packed his duffel. "You don't have to go with us."

He smiled. "I know."

Claire returned the expression and then bit her lip when he looked away. There wasn't really time for her to be going through some romantic crisis. It wasn't fair to Alex. It was distracting and exhausting and frustrating. What was wrong with her? Why couldn't she just make a decision about him? Was she making this more difficult than it needed to be? Maybe she already knew what she should do but couldn't bring herself to do it. But how could she be sure? Her head and her heart were warring with each other, and victory was nowhere in sight. She loved him, at least she used to. Was what she felt now still love? Or was it pity? Was all of this just some sense of obligation to him?

She watched him fold another shirt and stuff it into his bag, then run a hand through his messy hair. An ache filled her heart in the form of memories. Holding hands and walking under the stars. Running into the shelter of a nearby awning when it had started to rain. That first kiss with wet hair plastered to her cheek. It still felt like love. Maybe that was the problem. She loved him, but love wasn't enough anymore. Had love alone ever really been enough?

"Have everything you need?" Alex's question broke her out of her self-examination.

"Yeah, I'm good." She smiled at him again. The curve of her lips falling as he started to walk out of the room. "Alex," she called, stopping him at the door. He turned to her, brows raised. "Thank you…for everything."

He nodded a silent response and then left to go load their luggage into the car.

"Could you be any more awkward?" Zoe said as she dropped her carry-on to the floor.

"Probably not, but you could be more supportive."

"I think we are beyond the supportive phase and moving into the tough love phase. You need to get a grip," Zoe said and patted Claire's shoulder. "And I mean that from the deepest place of support and loving concern for your well-being."

"I'm sure, in time, I will come to appreciate that. But for now, we have a plane to catch. Got your passport?" Claire checked her own backpack one last time.

"Check."

Claire put her internal discussion on pause, focusing instead on their current task as she headed for the door. "Then let's go. We're going to swing by and pick up Daniel on the way."

"What about Michael?" Zoe called from behind.

"He's making his own travel arrangements." Claire held the front door open to let Zoe pass and made sure it was locked up behind them.

"Too good to fly coach with the common folk?" Zoe said and giggled.

"Scared of planes." Claire put on her sunglasses, stepped past Zoe and off the porch.

* * *

"How is an angel scared of flying?" Daniel whispered while they were boarding.

"It's not the flying, it's the plane. He gets claustrophobic or something," Claire said over her shoulder as she handed the attendant her boarding pass.

"That makes absolutely no sense to me."

"I stopped trying to make sense of Michael a long time ago," she said.

Claire found her seat, stuffed her duffel in the overhead compartment, and plopped down next to the window. Daniel and Zoe were in the row behind her. They had stowed their bags and settled in. Alex had taken the spot next to her. He had been silent almost the entire trip. She wasn't sure if it was Michael, or the nature of their excursion, or just her that had him so quiet. He seemed to be weighing something out. It was the same look he used to get whenever he was plotting out a photo shoot or making an important decision. She wondered if he was reevaluating his feelings for her as well. That thought made her stomach clench. Would it make things easier or harder if he were the one to walk away?

Claire slouched down in her seat and sighed heavily. How had this gotten so confusing?

Alex touched her knee. "Are you all right?"

"I hate long flights." It wasn't an excuse. It was true. The long flight provided too much time to think about things that she didn't want to think about. *What am I supposed to do?* Her mind screamed the silent question up to Heaven as the plane taxied to the runway.

* * *

A warm breeze blew through the open window, tossing the curtains. Birds were chirping somewhere out in the lush green of a spring day. Claire had gotten up early to fight the international time zones that separated her from her family and to make her weekly phone call to Zoe. She sat on the fire-escape and watched the sunrise as she caught up on their lives.

After hanging up, she stretched and yawned and realized she could sneak in at least another thirty minutes of sleep before work. So she climbed back in the window, the wood floors creaking under her bare feet. She pulled the down comforter back and climbed into the soft bed, snuggling close to Alex and wrapping her arms around him. She leaned her head against his shoulder and closed her eyes as she breathed in the sweet scent of his faded cologne.

Claire smiled against his bare skin. She couldn't remember the last time she'd felt this happy, this content with her life. It was like all the pieces had fallen together to create the picture she had always longed for—the fairytale, the happily-ever-after. Everything about this moment was perfect: the day, the apartment, the man beside her.

She took another long, deep breath of him, the sweetness tickling her nose, but this time something else was left behind, something sickening and familiar that irritated her senses. It couldn't be. That was all done; they were finished with the closing of Hell's gates, and saving the world, and fulfilling prophecies. Claire opened her eyes, not sure what she would find slinking in her room. There was nothing. It was just as pristine as it had been a moment ago, but the contented feeling was gone, concern taking its place.

It's just my mind playing some trick. Claire tried to shoo away the fear that was pricking at her brain with another inhale. She focused on the reality in front of her. She watched the rise and fall of Alex's chest, and it brought her own breath back into a calmer rhythm. She let her fingers trace the length of his arm. Alex twitched under her touch and she paused, not wanting to wake him, but it was too late. He reached his other hand to touch hers, so she leaned in and kissed his jaw. When he started to turn toward her, she laid back against her pillow and smiled at his face. His eyes were still closed, fighting for more sleep.

He kissed her nose in what seemed to her a sweet, sleepy accident. "Is it even morning yet?" His voice was a rough whisper.

"It is. Even the sun is up." Claire turned over to check the actual time on the bedside table.

She barely had enough time to register the numbers on the clock before she was pulled back into Alex's embrace. "Tell it to go back to bed and give me ten more minutes," he groaned softly.

"I don't think that's how it works." Claire snuggled against him, happiness seeping back into her veins.

Alex wrapped his arms tighter around her, holding her against his chest. "Any chance we can go back to the honeymoon then?"

"Of course."

"Another reason why I love you," he muttered sleepily.

"I love you, too." Claire smiled again and wiggled her way back to facing him. She brushed her hand through his hair.

Alex pulled her hand to his lips and planted a gentle kiss on her palm. His eyes opened.

Claire jerked her hand away and gasped. Solid black orbs were staring at her, and her heart felt like it had crashed against her chest and then stopped completely. "No." The word barely made its way out of her closing throat.

"Claire, what's wrong?" Alex caressed her cheek with his hand. Its icy chill burned her cheek.

"No!" Claire screamed out, jerking herself awake. She looked around confused, then remembered they were on the plane. Even though she realized she must have been dreaming, she brought her hand to her cheek, fully expecting to feel the tender mark of a burn.

"Claire, what's wrong?" Alex had shifted in his seat and was trying to comfort her, but she pushed him away.

"Aunt Claire?" Zoe's and Daniel's heads appeared over the top of her seat.

Claire blinked away the images from her dream until she had fully come back to her senses. "I'm fine. It was just a bad dream."

"Bad or *bad*?" Zoe's brow arched emphasizing the last bad.

"Normal bad. It's fine. I'm fine." Claire nodded her assurances until Zoe and Daniel were satisfied enough that they retreated back into their seats. "Sorry." She touched Alex's hand. She half expected it to feel cold, but it didn't.

"It's okay as long as you are," He said and smiled.

It was the first real smile he had given her in days. The goosebumps started to crawl over her skin the way they had the first time she had seen that smile. She wanted to drown in it. To forget everything and let herself fall all over again. Then something seemed to click inside him. The squint of his eyes gave away a hint of discomfort. He patted her hand and the curve of his mouth straightened as he looked away from her and back to the magazine he had been reading.

Claire felt a chill again, but it drew a different kind of sensation over her body this time. She shivered and stared at the gray sky out her window.

CHAPTER FOURTEEN

Maggie had created a second home for herself in the corner of Charlie's hospital room. She had the books from her homework reading list piled on the small table. She had a tote bag filled with snacks because she refused to eat in the cafeteria. Her phone was plugged into its charger so she wouldn't lose her connection to those traveling to the other side of the world. Maggie herself was sitting in the muted-blue vinyl recliner, wrapped in a fleece blanket and watching daytime television.

The beep of the heart monitor played consistently in the background of the soap opera she was getting sucked into. Every fifteen minutes, another machine would check Charlie's blood pressure. And once an hour, a nurse would come in, write something down, smile at her sadly, and then leave again. About a hundred times, she would swear she saw Charlie twitch out of the corner of her eye, but when she would look over, there would be no cause for any excitement. He was stable. That was the word the doctor had used when he'd stopped by on his daily rounds. It was all a waiting game, and Maggie was prepared to wait as long as she needed to, or at least until visiting hours were over at nine.

"I'll be back first thing in the morning," she whispered, kissing

Charlie on the cheek before the nurses politely kicked her out for the night.

* * *

Maggie was true to her word. The night sky was still fading, pushed back by the dim morning light of the dawn, when she walked through the hospital's automatic doors the following day.

"Good morning." Maggie yawned, failing at her effort to be bright and chipper in her greeting. She set a basket of muffins at the nurses' station. "Blueberry." She answered their unspoken question then continued down the hall to the fourth door on the right.

The room was the same. The beeping was the same. Charlie was the same.

"It'd be real nice if you woke up today, old man." She took off her coat and scarf and hung them on the door hook.

"Who you callin' old?" Charlie's rough voice scratched out in a dry whisper.

Maggie jerked toward the bed, unsure if she had really heard what she thought she'd just heard.

Charlie blinked. She watched as he cautiously lifted his hand and scratched at the tape holding the IV in his other arm.

Maggie was frozen, unable to move away from the door. For the first time in a very long while, she had nothing to say. What do you say to someone who's just woken up from a coma? Hi? Welcome back? Never do that again? All seemed like viable options at the moment, and yet none of them would actually make their way from her brain out of her mouth. So she just stared.

"Well, are you just gonna stand there?" Charlie tilted his head toward her.

As soon as his eyes connected with hers, she melted back into the reality of the moment and raced forward, threw herself against the bed, and gave Charlie a hug and a kiss on his cheek.

Charlie gently patted Maggie's back. "Easy, darlin'. Don't want to disconnect anything and send those nurses into panic."

Maggie sat up, wiping her eyes. Charlie's face seemed to have gained more color in just the past few seconds. She was happy to see a warm smile start to spread from his mouth up to his eyes. "You've had us all a little worried."

"Just a little?" He winked at her. "Speaking of us—where is everyone else? You my official babysitter?"

"We've all been taking shifts but I'm all you get for the next couple days at least," she told him. "The others are traipsing through the Middle East looking for swords and what not."

"So I take it they got the map back and figured out what it led to?" Charlie asked, trying to push himself forward so that he could sit up.

"Yeah, they did, and they did." Maggie helped adjust his pillows. "Michael said the weapon the map leads to is called the Eden Sword. Hopefully getting it is less eventful than getting the map back was."

"So Michael's back, which is a good thing. Why do I feel like there is also a bad thing?" he asked.

Grief rose into Maggie's chest and then kept going until it pooled at the edges of her brown eyes. She pictured Lucas lying there, under that horse blanket, blood on his shoes. She didn't want to remember him like that. She had tried forcing herself to forget that scene. But it was that image which now rushed to the forefront of her mind. She was unable to stop it. Why did she have to be the one here for this? Why should she have to bear the burden of telling Charlie the truth? But they all had their burdens, and if this one was hers, she would gladly bear it. She would be the curator of Lucas's heroism.

Maggie breathed in deeply, trying to somehow gain courage from the Lysol-scented hospital air so she could actually say the words to Charlie. "I wasn't there. But I know what they told me. I know you would have been proud of him."

"Of who?" Worry wrinkled Charlie's forehead.

"Lucas. He saved Claire. He probably saved them all." Maggie could feel the tears dripping down her cheeks and following the outline of her jaw. She cried all the way through sharing the rest of the tragic details.

When the nurses came in, she and Charlie let them believe their tears were tears of joy at his recovery. They watched in heavy silence as the nurses checked his vitals and called for the doctor.

"We're going to want to run some tests to be sure, but it looks like you'll be able to go home by tomorrow." Charlie nodded at the doctor's words.

Maggie smiled and whispered a polite thank you as he left the room.

Charlie touched her hand. "I'm going to need you to get something for me."

"Sure, anything," she said.

"There's a book in my trailer. My journal. It should be sitting on the counter, or maybe it's by my bed. Go grab it for me?"

Maggie giggled. "You need to express your feelings through writing?"

Charlie rolled his eyes. "No, I'm not gonna have a 'Dear Diary' moment. It's not that kind of journal. But it's got some information I need. I've got some calls to make."

CHAPTER FIFTEEN

Meredith sat at the bistro table outside the small market, fanning herself with a section of folded newspaper. "I still don't understand why we don't just grab the sword first. It's too hot to keep waiting around this dusty village. We beat them here, so let's just get the thing and go."

"I'm going to choose not to take your tirade as an insult to my intelligence," Abaddon said and sipped his tea. "I have told you before, we can't just go and take the sword from its current keeping. We need *her* for that."

Meredith used her napkins to dab the sweat from her forehead and the back of her neck. "Then can we please just kill her and get this whole thing over with? No Daughter, no weapon, no—"

"No Reaping, no fiery ending, no victory." Abaddon pounded his fist on the table making the glasses clink against their saucers, his eyes blazing. "Another Daughter will just rise. Killing Zoe now will merely delay things. I have waited too many millennia to get this close. I won't step backward because you can't stand a little heat."

Meredith swallowed hard and then leaned back in her chair,

trying to give the illusion of relaxation. "I'm sorry. I'm just afraid—"

"My dear, fear is *our* weapon. It is used on the weak, the unsure. I have seen inside that little girl's heart and she doesn't have the strength or the will to stop me. She will barely get to feel the sword's metal in her grip before we take it from her. Then she will most certainly die and my armies, which have been held back, waiting, will be unleashed on this world in their full force." He reached across the table for her hand. "You need not fear, love. This will all be over soon and we will not be the ones burning when it is done." Abaddon's lips grazed the top of her hand before he released it, returning to his reading and his tea.

* * *

Zoe handed her pack to Daniel, and he tossed it into the back of the rental car along with his. "So where exactly is Ur?" he asked.

"Under a few thousand years' worth of dirt," Alex answered. He followed suit with his own duffel and then Claire's.

Zoe hopped in the back seat. "So do we need shovels or…?"

Claire checked her phone screen. "No, there is already an archeological dig site pretty close to these coordinates that will hopefully give us some answers," she replied. "And Michael is already there."

"Goodie," Alex mumbled, hopping into the driver's seat.

"Can't Michael just, like, X-ray vision it all or something? Teleport us all to the right spot? I mean that would be helpful, am I right?" Daniel asked, sliding in next to Zoe.

"He's an angel—not a magic, comic-book superhero," Claire said with a chuckle. "Besides, I am sure the entrance to the trail is protected somehow, even from him. It has to be the Daughter who reveals the path, yada, yada."

"Well, don't I feel special?" Zoe tried to hide her anxiety with a small smile and a roll of her eyes. Neither stopped the nervous feeling that made her insides tremble. They had no idea what it would take from her to find the path, enter the garden, and take the sword. What if it meant using her powers? She wasn't sure she had enough faith in her powers, or herself for that matter. What would they think of her if they came all this way to stand in front of the instrument of the world's salvation and she couldn't even pick it up? What if she wasn't strong enough to pull the sword from the stone or whatever? *Please, help me.* Her heart pounded out her panicked prayer.

A warm tingle crawled down her arm and danced into her fingers. It was brief, so quick she was unsure if it was even real or just a trick her mind was playing on her. Was it the Maker, or simply the awakening of sleepy nerves and muscles after the long plane ride?

You need to hold on to something, Zoe. Just believe in it—choose to believe in it. If faith is a choice, then choose it. Zoe hoped her internal pep talk would be enough to keep her focused, to make it through this day, to open the door and allow her heart to start to truly heal. She wished for something more tangible, something she could grip tight with her feeble hands of faith. Couldn't there be something bigger, something that elevated all uncertainty, so that she could really know she wasn't forgotten?

The questions were already crumbling her resolve. She clenched her fists and tried to shove the doubts away.

* * *

A little more than an hour later, they came to a stop alongside some makeshift fencing. Michael was standing by the entrance to what Zoe guessed was the dig site Claire had mentioned.

"I think I have found something." The Guardian didn't even give them time to get out of the vehicle before speaking.

"Anyone else here?" Alex asked, shutting his door.

"No, it appears the site has been closed for some time," Michael replied.

Zoe took out her phone, checked for a signal, and then texted Maggie.

We're here. I'll keep you posted.

It only took a few seconds for Maggie's reply to chime.

Good. Watch out for booby traps and Nazis.

Zoe laughed out loud and typed her response.

This isn't an Indiana Jones movie, Mags.

"What?" Daniel asked, his weight pressing slightly against Zoe as he leaned close to read the texts over her shoulder. "Probably don't need to worry about Nazis, but she might not be wrong about the traps thing. As long as there aren't any snakes. I hate snakes." He chuckled.

"Really? You're getting as bad as Lucas." As soon as she said his name, she tensed.

Daniel's fingers were tangled with hers in seconds. "It's okay to talk about him," he said. "I mean, you're right. He totally would have made the snake joke."

Zoe swallowed and her muscles relaxed. "Totally." She squeezed his hand in gratitude before letting go, but a thought struck and she grabbed his arm again. "You don't think there will really be snakes, do you?"

"Snakes will be the least of our worries, I'm sure." Zoe let him kiss her cheek before they grabbed their bags and followed the others past the mesh barrier.

They followed a narrow path around the marked grid, each square revealing its own unique depths and layers of earth and history. It all seemed so much larger than these things ever did in the movies. An entire ancient city was being uncovered one block at a time. Soon they were no longer walking solid ground but atop the sketchy stone walls.

"Careful," Claire called out. Zoe watched as a few small rocks crumbled beneath her aunt's steps.

"Are you sure you're heading the right way?" Alex asked. "Wouldn't the ziggurat, a holy site, be a more likely place?"

"It would not," Michael replied. They all followed him in the opposite direction of the pyramid toward a southern corner of the excavation.

The further they walked, the deeper into the earth the path took them. Soon they were no longer on the walls, but surrounded by them as they stretched upward, blocking the afternoon sun. Zoe stepped carefully over the rougher terrain and down the remnant of steps which took them into a tight alleyway and then into a dark room at the outskirts of what had once been Ur.

Michael's blue eyes were glowing in the darkness. "Here," the angel said pointing at the corner.

Zoe followed the beam of Claire's flashlight which shone on a large stone, out of place among the smaller mud bricks that made up the wall. "What is that?" she asked, dusting her hand over the surface where symbols had been etched into the rock.

"Hebrew?" Alex had leaned in to get a closer look.

"It is older than Hebrew, and not a language written by men," Michael said. When he touched his finger to the chiseled characters, they slowly began to ignite into the same blue that illuminated the Guardian's veins, but then quickly faded back to just dark stone.

Zoe stepped forward, her legs shaking and her hands trembling. "Do you know what it says?" she asked.

Michael's eyes softened. "At the door to the beginning you will find the deliverance of the end," he answered.

Zoe stared hard at the words. Her chest heaved and hurt. "What do we do?"

"I do not know," Michael said as he continued to study the engraving.

Zoe was bumped out of the way by Daniel as he moved in closer.

"He touched it and it glowed," he said.

"But then it stopped," Alex added.

"But the Daughter is the only one who can reveal the path, so maybe you have to touch it," Daniel whispered to Zoe. She felt his fingers interlacing with hers.

Zoe swallowed. She turned from Daniel to Claire, who nodded her agreement and encouragement. "Okay, then." She closed her eyes and reached her hand out to the dust-covered rock. With the tips of her fingers, she could feel the lines that had been cut into the hard surface, but that was all she felt. Was anything even happening? *Please.* She squeezed her eyes closed and gripped Daniel's hand more tightly.

"Whoa," Daniel whispered.

Zoe peeked through one eye. The etchings were glowing, this time bright and white, filling in every carving and not fading like they had with Michael. Zoe's muscles relaxed as she released the breath she had been holding hostage.

As the last of the markings illuminated, the stone began to shake, its trembling tossing off centuries of dust. The white light behind the symbols spread out beyond their lines until the whole stone radiated with the same white glow. It grew brighter, burning Zoe's eyes. Then, as suddenly as it had appeared, it was gone and so was the stone.

"I guess we go that way now," Claire said pointing to the newly visible pathway.

Zoe's eyes were tired from straining to see in the dim space, and her legs and back were starting to hurt from ducking through the low rock formations. They had been following the path for awhile, and it was beginning to feel like it was going nowhere.

"Anyone wanna guess how deep this rabbit hole goes?" Alex asked as he ducked under another low rock. "If the ceiling gets any lower, we'll have to crawl."

"I think we're getting closer," Claire said. "Look, there's an opening ahead."

The cavernous ceiling began to rise, and as they passed through the opening, Zoe realized they were able to stand upright. The oil lamps, which lined the walls, began to light with small flames.

"Well, that's cool. And a little cliché," Daniel whispered in

Zoe's ear from behind her. "You sure we aren't in an Indiana Jones movie?"

Zoe giggled but it was more nervous than anything. They were so close; she could feel it. She didn't know how, but she could, like something was pulling her. She wanted to stop, to turn around and run back into the sunlight and back home. More than once during this underground hike, she'd tried, but something had kept tugging her forward. So she would keep moving and keep hoping it was a good sign.

Their path curved around a bend and into a large open chamber. There were no more lamps and no need for flashlights because light streamed in like the sun shining on a summer day. It descended from somewhere above, a great beam directed at a large tree at the center of the room. It sparkled off the leaves which reflected the dancing light throughout the chamber.

"How is that even possible?" Alex asked, rubbing at the back of his neck.

"Possible is a relative term," Claire answered.

"I've seen it before," Zoe muttered.

"What? When?" Claire looked at her, then back to the tree.

"In my dreams." Zoe could feel the smile playing at the corners of her mouth. A new confidence tickled through her skin and began to percolate into her heart. She dropped her pack and walked closer to the tree with its familiar gnarled branches and heavy roots. She was nearly within reach of it when the ground began to shake. Two stone obelisks rose up and blocked her way. Zoe stumbled back.

"Zo!" Daniel yelled. He reached for her, but a blinding light surged from the pillars.

Zoe covered her face against the brightness, but then she felt it. The warmth was flowing in her veins, out from her heart, down her arms to her tingling fingers and back up, pooling behind her eyes. She blinked once and the light wasn't bright anymore, at least not to her. She glanced back to see the others still squinting, shielding their faces behind their hands and arms. All except

Michael, who stood statuesquely. His eyes were blazing blue and focused on the light. Zoe returned her own gaze to it. She watched it swell, and then it seemed to squeeze into an orb. She gasped. There was something in it, something moving. She felt the tug again, pulling her forward, closer. There it was, the Eden Sword, spinning inside the ball of light, white-hot flames engulfing it. There were no instructions, no voice telling her what to do, but she knew. Some hidden instinct took over and she reached her hand out before she could consider that it might be a bad idea. The closer she got to the orb, the stronger its pull became, drawing her in until her fingers broached its edge. The sword stopped turning just as she was within reach. She wrapped her hand around its grip. It was large, the blade longer than she was tall, and it felt too heavy, but she couldn't let go. She wouldn't let go. She pulled the daunting weapon from the light and watched as it shrank to an ideal size. Holding it now, it was like it had been forged just for her, the perfect height, weight, and balance.

The white light began to fade between the pillars and in Zoe's eyes. The flames coming off the sword died down, leaving it shimmering like pure gold in her hands.

A slow clap echoed off the stone walls of the cavern. "Well, well, well. Look at you and your fancy new toy."

Zoe scanned the room, settling her gaze on the black eyes. He was standing near the entrance, watching her. "Abaddon."

Claire had already dropped her pack and was lifting her sword to the ready. "You won't get that weapon or hurt her."

Meredith slinked into view. "Are you sure?" she asked.

"How dare you defile this place." Electricity began to surge down Michael's arms, creating his silver blade.

"Sorry to tell you, I defiled this place a long time ago. I have to say, it was more impressive back then." Abaddon smirked. He began to walk closer.

Zoe found herself suddenly surrounded by Claire, Michael, and Daniel. A chill traced her spine. She shivered.

"What's the matter Zoe? Not feeling so capable?" Abaddon

asked. "But you have the instrument of my demise right there in your little hands—you should be dying to use it." The Destroyer lifted his hand, emitting smoke which stretched and formed into a cutlass.

"Or she could just die," Meredith scoffed.

"Can we skip the snarky banter?" Claire asked.

Zoe watched as Meredith sauntered closer to Alex and ran her hand over his shoulder. "Your girlfriend is getting cranky," she said to him.

"Alex, be careful." Claire had moved forward but halted with a gasp when Alex's eyes swirled to black.

"You don't need to worry about me," he said with a crooked grin.

Claire's grip faltered and her sword lowered, hanging loose at her side. "No, this isn't you. How?"

Alex laughed. "Oh sweetie, I went to Hell, remember? I was never really that good."

"Heaven and Hell aren't about you being good. I know things have been hard but it doesn't have to be this way—you could be different," Claire said in a shaky voice.

"Maybe, if you hadn't abandoned me, lied to me, and pushed me aside again and again." Alex's tone became colder with each word.

Zoe's own tears began to blur her vision as she watched her aunt's hand shake, the quiver rattling all the way to the tip of her sword. "Aunt Claire?"

Claire turned toward Zoe as if the quiet plea had woken her up. Her lips tightened and her brow wrinkled. She lifted her sword back into proper fighting form and turned back to address Alex. "Your choices are all your own. Maybe I could have done some things differently, but you choosing to become *this*, I won't be blamed for it."

"I hate to interrupt—I do love a good heartbreak, and dear Claire, yours is shattering—but we have business to attend to. Make this easy on yourselves and just give me the sword...and the

Daughter." Abaddon snapped his fingers and sneered. "Would it help if I said pretty please?"

A low rumble echoed down the cave's corridor. The walls rattled as a pack of hellhounds appeared, leading hundreds of demons down the ancient path into the chamber. Zoe braced herself for a fight. She squinted as lightning burst out of Michael's back and stretched into large wings.

"You will take neither," the Guardian said. His voice, so full of authority and empty of fear, was comforting to Zoe.

"We'll see," said Abaddon. The ranks of demons came pouring into the chamber past the Destroyer, charging toward the descendants.

The horde of shadows swarmed like a thick, black cloud around them. Zoe could barely see Claire and Daniel fighting through the throng. The luminescent blue of Michael's wings flashed between the dark silhouettes of the death dogs. Zoe did her best to beat down every beastly creature that came her way. She could feel their icy presence all around her, the cold of their touch searing into her consciousness. The chill was occasionally interrupted by the warmth of the light underneath her flesh. When its heat danced down her skin, she did her best to concentrate on the sensation, begging it to pour out of her and tear down the darkness. It began to brighten, glowing past her fingertips and disintegrating the demon in front of her. Faith began to rise up steadily, its strength fortifying her stance. With a renewed vigor, she attacked fiercely at the demons thrashing about her.

There were too many. Power was returning in her veins, growing stronger with every step,

but it was nowhere near what she needed to obliterate the mass surrounding them. She could hear Michael calling for Claire, making sure she was all right. She could hear Daniel groan in pain and then growl in attack. *Help!* Zoe wasn't sure if the prayer was silent or if she had actually shouted it, but the shadows began to draw back. For a moment her chest lightened. But it was just a moment, then her lungs constricted again. Abaddon was walking

69

toward her, his weapon in hand. The demons had only been clearing a path for their master.

Zoe bit her lip and clenched the grip of her new sword with her sweaty palms. She lifted it, ready to strike at her enemy, but she couldn't hide the fear which made her arms and legs wobble.

Abaddon leered at her weak attempt. "Make this easier on yourself, on them."

"Zoe!" Claire's voice called through the swarm. "I'm coming!"

"No, she isn't." Meredith's voice was a sickening song before Zoe heard the metal swords clanging together.

Zoe trembled as the Destroyer came closer and the hounds howled.

"You can stop all of this, Zoe." Abaddon took another step.

Zoe shook her head slowly. She heard Daniel cry out and jerked her head, trying to see him, but glimpses of the white of his t-shirt were all she could make out.

"Come on, Zoe. No one else has to die," Abaddon said, lifting his sword.

Zoe gripped hers tighter, readying herself to strike.

Abaddon quickened his pace, preparing to lunge at her.

A loud cracking sound broke through the hiss of the demons. The shadows shrieked and slunk backward. Cobalt light fractured the obelisks. The stones broke into two large figures which uncurled marble arms as they rose from their perches. Electricity flowed beneath their surface, striking out to form wings and swords. They looked akin to Michael but larger, and as they turned and stood, their wings, six each, lifted and stretched wide. The beings stepped down. Sparks of power began emitting from them both and struck down the shadows in waves.

Michael, Claire, and Daniel closed ranks around Zoe again as Abaddon roared. They watched him retreat back, exclaiming, "I am not finished!"

Meredith and Alex joined him, and they all dissolved into smoke and disappeared.

When all the ashes had settled and the light was restored in full measure, the seraphim returned to their stone pedestals. One set of their wings wrapped around them while the others extended, forming a wall from the chamber's floor to ceiling. Their blue light crackled as what had been pliable once again became stone. The creatures had created a partition which blocked the tree and hid the light, leaving Zoe and the others in a darkness that was only barely dissolved by the dim light of the oil lamps just outside the chamber doors.

"Are you okay?" Zoe felt Claire's arm wrap around her.

She responded with a silent nod.

"Then let's go home." Claire hugged her.

"We may need to take a minute." Daniel was standing beside Michael, whose hand was clutching his side.

"I will be fine," Michael muttered, then dropped to one knee, blood oozing through his fingers.

CHAPTER SIXTEEN

The clack of Meredith's heels echoed through the sparse warehouse and Alex's head as he followed her inside.

"We failed. All of the time and planning, and we barely got within reach of it." Meredith stomped harder with each word. "Those cherubim would not have been so formidable if you had faced them in your true form."

Alex watched as Abaddon poured himself a cup of Earl Grey. He stirred in one cube of sugar, his spoon clinking against the porcelain. He took a sip then sat down on his antique chair, setting the cup on the side table next to a stack of old books. "There you go again, love, insulting me," he said, addressing Meredith's complaint. "Didn't I promise you they would all burn?"

"Yes...b-but..." Meredith stammered.

The dichotomy between the two confused Alex. Meredith seemed on edge, tense, her eyes flitting over the floor. Abaddon was calm, relaxed, as he chose a book from his pile and flipped through it as if he were finding his page.

Abaddon glanced over his reading. "Love, you're making the boy tense. You should both relax. Get something to eat, go see a movie, whatever it is humans do to fill their miserable existence."

"What about the sword? Zoe?" Alex puffed up his chest, offended at being called boy. "I thought we were going to finish this. That's what you promised *me*." He pressed his palms into the table that sat in the center of the makeshift room.

Abaddon closed his book, keeping his finger tucked between the pages. He sat up and moved to the edge of his seat. "My apologies. It seems you both had certain expectations of today and that is my fault. I've kept things from you, important things, but it's time for you to understand. Today wasn't a setback. It was a setup."

"But I thought the goal was to get the sword?" Alex was tired of riddles and half-truths. He wanted to see all the pieces of the puzzle.

Abaddon's jaw clenched, making his words sound hard. "The goal is domination. The goal is ultimate victory. The goal is to make the Maker pay by destroying everything He loves. The sword and the girl are pawns, an annoying necessity."

"But you wanted the sword," Meredith said, her brow furrowing.

"Yes, and I will have it. But the sword does nothing without the girl. I must be sure that when she stands at the gates of Hell, her heart is oh so very broken and weary and angry." Abaddon growled out each word with a twisted grin. "She can be the instrument of my destruction or my victory. I told you before, killing her only delays things. I need her to walk out her destiny, but I need her to lose sight of why. So you see, today wasn't a defeat. It was a small victory. The tools of my triumph are in play. She still doubts herself. And what I've done to the Guardian, along with what I will do to each of her pitiful family members, will solidify those doubts and fears. The scales are tipped in our favor, and we will make sure they stay that way."

"How?" Alex leaned in, hanging on the Destroyer's every word. He had seen what had been done to Michael. The hellhound controlled by Abaddon had bitten its poisonous fangs right into the angel's side. For a brief moment, Alex had felt sickened by it, sorry even. Then he had remembered Michael and Claire sitting on the porch together, and envy frosted his veins and iced over any sympathy he had left.

Abaddon took another sip of his tea then smirked. "With blood and pain."

CHAPTER SEVENTEEN

"How did this happen?" Claire held the linen scarf she had been wearing against Michael's wound.

"What do you need us to do?" Zoe asked over her shoulder.

"Look through the packs and get the first aid supplies, bandages, antiseptic, whatever we brought."

"We didn't bring much. He was our first aid plan A," Daniel said, coming up alongside them.

"I told you, I will be fine." Michael grabbed Claire's hand.

She bit her bottom lip to still its shaking. "I have never seen you hurt like this."

They had spent almost two decades together. They had fought demons, slain praetors. She had seen him bleed. It was rare, only happening when they'd taken on a particularly nasty and unusually large opponent. It had never been like this. By the time he would have wiped the blood away, his wound would have been healed. And while she had seen him tired and sore, he had never appeared weak. But now he could barely stand. The bleeding wasn't stopping, and she watched him wince with every inhale. Her own breathing was growing more labored as her body betrayed her. Her muscles were unexpectedly feeble and her limbs too heavy, making it difficult for her to act.

Michael moved his hand to her neck, tucking his fingers between loose strands of her hair. His thumb brushed against her cheek. "It was a hound. Its poison is making the healing process slower, but I will heal."

"I can't lose you. Abaddon knows it." She felt her fear turn to tears that stuck behind her thick lashes. "This is more than just the risk of battle being realized. This was a strategic maneuver."

Michael winced yet again, then said, "Perhaps he meant to kill me. I would think he hoped his hounds would get more than one bite in before the cherubim appeared. But they did not."

"He knew the cherubim would help us?" Zoe asked, kneeling down next to Claire with the first aid kit.

"I believe he did." A grimace twisted across the Guardian's face as Claire pulled the scarf away to take another look at his wound. "Or at least he accounted for the possibility."

Claire was having a hard time caring. It didn't matter if this was all part of Abaddon's plans or not. In an hour, a day, she would feel differently. She knew it. She knew they would have to think all this through and try to get two steps ahead of their enemy. But now, right now, in the dim light of millennia-old oil lamps, she only cared about Michael.

She scolded herself for that thought. She cared about Daniel and Zoe and the sword, and Alex turning into a monster. *Alex.* She cared so much about all of it, but she didn't want to. She wanted to help Michael. She wanted to know that he was going to be okay. She wanted to get out of this place. She wanted to be home and safe, and she didn't want to be alone.

Where did that come from? Her mind was racing, trying to keep pace with her panicked heart. She wasn't alone. But she had been once, and for some reason, the fear that she would be again was crippling her focus. That was it. That was what the Destroyer was doing. He was pulling tiny strings, one at a time, until they unraveled. It started with Lucas the day of the parade. Again when

Daniel got hurt, and then Charlie. He had almost succeeded when Lucas died, but it was really just another little string.

Claire did her best to clean Michael's wound while her head whirled. She wrapped bandages tight around his torso. This was another string. The Destroyer was pulling at the little pieces of their love and security and faith. She knew it, but knowing it didn't stop her undoing. Her soul was weakening, and finding the right thread to tie it all back together seemed suddenly impossible.

Blood started to seep through Michael's bandages. "We need to get home," she said. She tucked a loose strand of hair behind her ear and helped Michael to stand.

"Do not get lost in your worry." Michael's whisper was warm against her ear.

She knew he had meant for his words to encourage her, but they only heightened her fears. She had spent too long depending on him to lose him. She needed Michael. She shouldn't. She hated herself for how she felt about him. Her soul was tethered to his, and whether it was meant to or not, it bound them together in a way they could not break free of. He leaned his weight on her shoulder and she felt her own weakness growing. She wasn't her without him. She didn't know if she even could be.

CHAPTER EIGHTEEN

"Do we really need to do this?" Charlie couldn't see where he was going through the green needles and his stomach was growling with hunger like it was trying to play catch up for all the missed meals over the past few weeks.

"It's Christmas. They will be home in less than an hour. Yes, we need to do this," Maggie replied.

Together, they maneuvered the heavy, sticky tree toward the corner of the living room by the front window.

Charlie grunted as he set the trunk into its stand. "I'm just saying, based on what they told you, I don't think they'll be in the Christmas spirit, darlin'."

Maggie, her hands on her hips, was staring at the tree. She tilted her head and squinted her eyes. She looked like she was plotting something. "Which is why they need us to get them into the spirit," she said. "Christmas is non-negotiable. Now you go get the decorations out of the attic and I'll bake the cookies."

"You do remember I was just in a coma in the hospital like two days ago, right?"

"It was like you had a really long nap. You're fine." Maggie dropped her coat and gloves on the sofa. "The boxes aren't even heavy, I checked it all out earlier."

"But you didn't think to bring them down?" Charlie asked.

"And deprive you of contributing?"

"I would've survived." Charlie adjusted his hat and obeyed Maggie's orders. He might have complained the entire time they were at the tree lot—to be fair, it should not take two hours to choose a tree when they all look exactly the same—but this was a good idea. He couldn't remember the last time he had anything resembling a real Christmas, unless eating a microwave turkey dinner while watching *It's A Wonderful Life* on a tiny television alone in your RV counted. There were times, years ago, when the descendants would gather and make the time to celebrate together. When was the last time they had done that? It had to have been right after whispers of the Daughter had started circulating, when they'd all thought it was Claire... so it had been a long time. After that, things had gotten harder; demonic activity had intensified. They were spread too thin, too tired for the extra effort of holidays and funerals.

Being so tired was why they'd doubted Claire. She wasn't the Daughter, but they hadn't known that. They'd just known she was off doing her own thing, not caring about their plight. Charlie wished he could go back, bring them the truth, and tell them she needed them. Would things have been different if they hadn't been self-pitying and selfish, but rather had reached out to her when she didn't know they were there for her to reach? He was here now, and they would be too. You can't go back, but you can make things right moving forward. Claire and Zoe would have an army behind them to face the army before them. They weren't going to be alone, not on his watch.

CHAPTER NINETEEN

Claire stood on one side of Michael and Daniel was on the other, helping her get the guardian up the porch steps. "Do you smell cookies?" Daniel asked.

The sweet aromas of sugar cookies, cinnamon, and pine all mixed together and filtered from the house. They mingled in Claire's nose with the scent of a coming snow. Snow on Christmas had always felt magical to her. It had been a long time since she was in a climate where it was even a possibility. Circumstances were keeping her from enjoying the thrill of it this year. Was it even Christmas already? She had known it was coming, but all the trappings had gotten lost in war and grief. The holiday crooning that floated out felt like the wrong soundtrack to be playing in the background of their present scene.

Zoe jumped in front of her, twisted the knob, and pushed the door open. "Is that Michael Bublé?" she asked. "Whatever this is, it has Maggie written all over it."

No sooner had they stepped inside than the scene began to change. There was a fire crackling in the fireplace below a garland draped mantle. Candles were lit on the coffee table. A spruce tree was in the corner and boxes spilling over with ornaments and decorations littered the floor.

"I thought you guys would never get home," Maggie said as she came into view wearing felt reindeer antlers and a green and red plaid apron. "Did you get the sword?"

"Yeah, we did," Zoe replied as she unzipped her bag and pulled the Eden Sword into the light.

"Can I touch it?" Maggie asked.

"I don't see why not," Zoe replied.

Maggie approached the weapon with wide eyes, reaching her fingers out slowly and looking as though the thing would shock her if she were found unworthy or something. "This is way cool," Maggie said with a low whistle. "Where was it? Was it guarded by angels? Were there booby traps? Snakes? I want all the details." Maggie bounced in place. Her excitement was both refreshing and exhausting. Claire knew it was a big deal, but it wasn't a story any of them wanted to relive just yet.

"I'll tell you all about it later. I promise, Mags," Zoe said as she put the sword back in her oversized duffel.

"Sure," Maggie said and sighed. She seemed more than a little disappointed at first but snapped herself out of it with a new question. "Where's Alex?"

Claire felt her legs starting to go numb just a little, and she tightened her grip on Michael. "Let's save that story for another time, too." She took a second glance around the living room. "I'd rather talk about what you've been up to. You did all this?" she asked as she aided Michael to the couch.

"I had help." Maggie smiled and turned behind her. It was only then that Claire noticed Charlie, who was coming from the kitchen with a half-eaten cookie in hand. "I thought I told you not to touch those until we decorated them!" Maggie scolded him.

Claire laughed at Charlie, who stuffed the rest of the sugar cookie into his mouth, then shuffled past Maggie as she raised her hand to swat him but missed.

Daniel was quick to step up and give Charlie a fist bump. "Are there more?" he asked.

"Kitchen counter," Charlie said and chuckled.

"Don't even think about it!" Maggie warned Daniel. "First we eat dinner, then we decorate the tree, then we ice the cookies."

"Dinner? That works too! I'm starving." Daniel ran into the kitchen.

"What else is new?" Zo asked as she gave Charlie a quick hug on her way toward her friends and the kitchen.

"Those three are something," Charlie said, stepping in front of Claire.

"*Something* is right." Claire embraced the old man. "I have missed you," she whispered.

"Right back at ya." Charlie pulled away from her and stepped toward the fireplace. "If you're hungry, Maggie ordered Chinese— way too much Chinese."

"Maybe in a minute," Claire replied, sitting herself next to Michael who did a poor job of stifling his painful wince as he sat back.

"That bad?" Charlie asked.

"I have experienced worse," Michael answered.

"Not that I've ever seen." Claire checked his bandages again. She had checked them every thirty minutes, but there had barely been a change. The bleeding had slowed but the skin had yet to knit itself back together, which did nothing to ease her concerns.

Michael's hand brushed her knee as he said, "You have not known me my entire existence."

"I don't find that comforting," Claire muttered, letting Michael's plaid shirt fall back over his bloody bandages. "We need to replace those."

"I'm guessing taking an angel to the hospital wasn't an option?" Charlie's question briefly drew Claire's attention.

"They can do nothing more than Claire has already done," Michael said, his hand once again warming a spot on her knee. Claire patted it, then stood back up.

"Stitching you up in the airplane lavatory was an experience I won't soon forget." She giggled at the thought of his large and panicking form trying to fit in the small space without putting a foot in the toilet.

Claire bit her lip to block another giggle as she watched her Guardian's face go slack. "I do not like planes."

Charlie laughed. "Claire, go get some food. I'll tend to the patient."

"You don't have to—"

"I'm not asking," Charlie interrupted. "You need to eat. Besides, either you go willingly, or Maggie is going to come out here and get you."

"I'm going." Claire held up her hands in surrender. She touched Michael's shoulder. He took her hand and squeezed it gently before letting it go so she could walk away. She took a couple of steps into the hall, then retreated back into the living room long enough to give Charlie a second hug. "It really is good to see you awake again, friend." She placed a sweet kiss on his scruffy cheek. "We need you around here."

* * *

One too many cartons of fried rice later and Claire's stomach hurt. The pain could have also been from laughter as they all dug through boxes of ornaments and memories. Decades of homemade decorations and horribly embarrassing throwback photos were enough for the Christmas spirit to break through.

"Look what I found!" Claire looked up from her nostalgia to see Daniel dangling a cluster of leaves over his head.

"Mistletoe? Really?" Zoe asked. One couldn't help but notice her cheeks grow a little rosier.

"Really, babe," Daniel replied. Claire dodged his clunky steps, trying to keep him from tripping over her as he made his way to Zoe with his eyes closed and his lips puckered.

Zoe giggled. "I'm going to ignore the babe thing."

Claire couldn't save Daniel from tripping over the box next to Zoe, who did catch him just in time for him to kiss her sweetly.

A camera shutter clicked. "I'm so posting that," Maggie said, her smart phone held in front of her and aimed at the cute couple.

"You're not," Zoe responded.

"I am," Mags taunted, "then I'm going to get a print made and frame it for you because it's adorable." Maggie smiled at the screen in her hand. The smile faltered, briefly but enough for Claire to notice a hint of sadness glaze her eyes.

Claire squatted next to her. "Thinking of Lucas?"

"Trying not to think of him actually. Christmas is supposed to be happy and merry and bright. Not mopey."

"Who says thinking of him has to be mopey?" Claire asked. She stared at her reflection in the shiny red ornament in her hand for a moment before adding, "He would have hated all this, and would have made sure we all knew it—with every sarcastic bit of commentary he could come up with."

Maggie chuckled. "No, he would have loved it, but acted like he hated it just to bug us all."

"I think he would have gotten super sappy and emotional," Zoe added, hanging a glittery ball on the tree.

Daniel handed her another ornament. "I cannot imagine a sappy Lucas. Snarky, yes. Sappy, no," he said.

Maggie wiped her eyes and her smile returned. "I agree with Zo. He was really a softy at heart."

"If we are going to go with this scenario, then I get to imagine making fun of him for being sappy," Daniel added.

Zoe rested a hand on her cocked hip. "No, you don't. I mean this probably would have been the first Christmas he would have celebrated since he was little," she said.

Claire and everyone else paused in what they were doing. The room was stalled by silence and sad faces. It was like Lucas's ghost had joined them. First it was making a joke about Daniel and the mistletoe and how hopeless he was. Then it was refusing to sing jingle bells with Maggie only to give in through a mouth stuffed with cookie. It asked to hang the star on the tree with sad puppy eyes and smiled from its seat on the sofa while they opened presents.

"Presents!" Claire put her hand over her mouth and gasped.

"It's okay, Aunt Claire," Zoe said and rubbed her eyes with the sleeve of her sweater. "With everything going on, we didn't really expect any presents."

"Oh, I bought presents—I just forgot I did," Claire said as she headed for the stairs.

"When did you have time to buy presents?" Zoe asked.

"I picked up things here and there for the past couple of months," Claire replied. "Why are you all so surprised? We've already established that I'm awesome."

Claire flashed them a last huge smile before running upstairs to retrieve packages from the back of her closet. Her hands were full when she stepped back into the room. "Sorry they aren't wrapped," she said, trying not to drop everything.

"You lose awesome points for that," Zoe said, punctuating her words with sassy wink.

"I'll live with that." Claire passed out the boxes. She watched each of them take turns lifting the lids and discovering what was inside. There was a new sketchbook and pencils for Maggie because Claire hadn't seen her draw in a while and thought it was time to start again.

"I know just what the first sketch will be," Maggie said as she flipped through the book's blank pages.

A leather-bound journal for Daniel because he had so much to offer in this fight, and she wanted him to share it.

He stared at Claire with wide eyes. "I don't know what to write," he said.

Claire reached out and touched his hand. "I have a feeling that once you start, you'll find you have a lot to say."

A bracelet for Zoe, wooden beads with a small charm which read *be brave*. "For when you need the reminder and I'm not there," Claire spoke softly to her niece as Zoe rubbed the beads between her fingers.

"Thank you," Zoe said, hugging Claire tight.

For Charlie, a wooden frame with a picture Maggie had made all of them take together at Thanksgiving.

"A picture?" The old man rolled his eyes with a playful scoff.

Claire smiled at him. "A family."

Charlie coughed, then adjusted his trucker hat, obviously choked up.

Claire stared at the remaining boxes in front of her. She had gotten a new camera for Alex. What should she do with it now? Could giving it to him unlock something that might pull him back from the precipice? Should she risk hoping? She couldn't think about him, not right now. She pushed the box aside with the other orphaned gift. She had scribbled "Lucas" across the top in messy cursive like she had on the others, thinking she would have gotten to wrap them with pretty paper and festive bows before giving them away. She didn't know why seeing his, with his name almost illegible, hurt. It did though. He deserved more. He deserved to have one more Christmas, at least. He deserved to have a lifetime of them, with a family who loved him. He didn't deserve a plain little box with messy handwriting. He didn't deserve to die for her. She held the box in her trembling hand.

"Do not go to that place," Michael said, his body suddenly brushing against hers, his hand on hers, steadying it.

"What did you get him?" Maggie asked, her question barely more than a shaky whisper.

Claire set the box back down. "I got him his own key to the house," she said. "I wanted him to know he had a home now."

"He knew," Michael assured her, his fingers tightening around her hand.

She swallowed back her heartache. "We weren't supposed to get mopey." Claire smiled up at the Guardian. "I got you something, too."

"You did not have to," he responded.

"Oh, I know. But that's the thing about gifts," Claire said, handing Michael the last box. Inside was a leather cuff with a metal plate engraved with three numbers. "It's the day we first met."

"I know." The angel slipped the bracelet onto his wrist. "It was a very significant day."

"It was." Claire couldn't tear her gaze away from her Guardian. She had forgotten anyone else was even watching them until Charlie coughed and drew her attention to the three teenagers staring at her, arched brows and toothy grins holding back their commentary. Her cheeks grew warm. She rubbed her hands along her thighs to dry her sweaty palms. "That's it for the presents," she said.

"Actually, there's one more." Charlie stood up. "Everyone come with me," he ordered.

* * *

Alex was leaning against the large metal doorway, looking up at the emerging stars. It was Christmas. He'd never really loved Christmas until he'd met Claire. They'd only spent one together, but it had been warm in all the ways you could imagine, and it was getting more and more difficult for him to remember anything warm. The air was getting colder as the sun fell, but the chill under his skin was greater than anything on the surface. It felt alarming and consoling all at once.

"You get used to it," Meredith said, joining him.

"I'm not sure if that's a good thing or not." He shoved his hands into his pockets.

He felt Meredith's fingers crawling over his shoulder and down his chest. Then she rested her head against him. "The regret you are feeling will fade," she said. "It's a weakness. One you'll be glad to be rid of."

"Will I? Will I ever really be rid of it?" he asked, not knowing if what he felt was hope or fear.

"The deeper you let him take you, the further you will be from humanity's emotional trappings."

Alex turned to face her. "Do you feel anything?"

Meredith's head tilted and her eyes peered deep into his. She grinned and licked her lips as she pulled at the collar of his jacket. "I feel power. I feel desire."

"What about love?"

A laugh erupted from the proselyte's throat. "Love is overrated. You'll come to see that. Trust me." Suddenly, her lips were pressing into his. He was surprised by how cold they were. Her hands were always cold, so much so that he could feel it through his t-shirt whenever she touched him. But he hadn't expected her lips to be icy as well. It was strange, but what was even stranger was how the cold was becoming familiar, like it had always been a part of him. It hadn't though, right? Did it matter? This was who he was now, who he had become, who *Claire* had forced him to be. *Claire*.

A memory, one with her smile, jumped into frame, bringing momentary warmth with it inside his chest, but it didn't last. The fondness quickly chilled to regret and guilt and anger and betrayal. Ice wrapped around his heart again, killing any spark that memory might have brought, preventing it from being fanned into flame. He kissed Meredith harder. She wasn't who he wanted, but maybe he had been wanting the wrong thing all along. Meredith was right. Love was an unnecessary weakness which gave nothing in return but pain. It wasn't worth it. He tangled his fingers in her black hair, tugging her closer. He needed to want her, to want anything but Claire. He needed to believe that living without her was better than not living at all. Both felt like hell.

CHAPTER TWENTY

What is Charlie up to? Zoe noted the sparkle in his eyes and a lightness in his step as he led her and the others out of the house.

"Where are we going?" Daniel asked, fumbling with his keys.

Charlie paused at his driver's side door. "My gift is waiting for you all back at the barn," he said with a wink.

Zoe leaned in close to Maggie so she could whisper in her ear, "Do you know what it is?"

"Not a clue," Maggie replied before sliding into Daniel's truck with her.

Zoe wasn't sure what to expect from the old man, and she probably wasn't the only one. After all, he had been in a coma for weeks, so it wasn't like he'd had a lot of shopping time. But even in their wildest imaginings, they would never have guessed the sight they found at the end of the gravel drive. A couple of vintage RVs were parked by Charlie's. A rusty Jeep Wrangler was next to the fence, and a couple more beat-up trucks were in the drive. Lights were on in the barn and music was drifting through the faded planks.

Zoe slowly exited the vehicle. She looked around to see the others staring at Charlie with the same confusion she felt. They all just stood there gaping, like they were all hesitant to investigate further.

"It's okay. No one's gonna bite," Charlie called over his shoulder as he walked to the barn doors and slid them open. A cheerful greeting erupted from inside which piqued Zoe's interest further.

"We won't know until we go inside," Claire said, smiling at them all. Then she and Michael led the way.

"It sounds like a party," Maggie said to Zoe, smiling wide and bouncing in place to the beat of the song which had now gotten louder thanks to the opened door.

"We could probably use one of those," Zoe said, grinning back at her. She took Daniel's hand and they all walked into the shelter of the aging barn.

Christmas lights had been strung from a section of the rafters. A table had been set up with a variety of foods, a small Christmas tree as its centerpiece. The music they had heard wasn't from the stereo but from two men who were sitting next to the training mats and playing guitars. Zoe counted another five or so people she didn't know mingling about. Some were singing, a couple were dancing, and all wore warm smiles.

"Who are all these people?" Zoe asked, stopping next to Claire.

"Descendants," Charlie replied.

"Why are they here?" Zoe watched them all glance from her to Claire, whispering between mouthfuls and dance steps.

Charlie tilted his head toward her. "For you. They came to help."

"You did this?" Claire asked.

"I didn't have to do much, and hopefully these won't be the last to come before the final fight," he said, grinning and clapping his hands together. "Well, you all gonna stand in the doorway all night, or let me introduce you around?" Charlie grabbed Zoe and Claire's hands and tugged them both forward. His first stop was the musicians. "These are the twins, Bobby and Billy. They're from Texas."

The two men, who didn't stop playing but only nodded and smiled in response to their introduction, looked to be just in their late twenties. They had matching blue eyes and brown beards.

Charlie kept tugging them along. There was a couple standing to the side, holding hands and tapping their feet to the music. They both had long black hair, with subtle touches of gray, and tanned skin. "This is Jack and Sue, the Walkers. They're usually found up in the Dakotas and Montana, but can occasionally be persuaded to travel," Charlie said, letting go of Zoe and Claire long enough to shake Jack's hand and pat his shoulder.

Sue reached a hand out to Claire. "Well, it isn't often Charlie calls. And to come and meet the Armor-Bearer and the Daughter—that's a first," she said, then let go of Claire and turned to Zoe. She didn't offer Zoe a handshake, but rather a warm embrace. "We're just sorry we weren't here sooner," she whispered in Zoe's ear, "if we had known…"

"You're here now." Zoe pulled back and smiled at Sue, hoping to conceal the tears that were threatening to spill over. She had never met this woman before but felt like she knew her, like she was family who had been long removed and now reunited. Joy pumped through her veins, a relief from the fear and grief. Hope was flooding in again, its warmth tingling through her nerves. They had help, and knowing that made her burden feel a little lighter.

Charlie continued to give names to the new faces and Zoe worried she wouldn't be able to keep them all straight. Thomas had been a pastor in the Midwest. His sister, Catherine, now fought with him. She was like Maggie in that her faith had opened her eyes to the true nature of the darkness around them. Levi, who looked to be around Charlie's age with his dark skin wrinkling around his eyes, was Rufus's son. Claire had been so excited to hear the name of her grandfather's old companion from the journals. She kept Levi trapped by a plate of cookies for nearly an hour asking questions about his father and her grandfather.

Zoe felt somehow outside of herself, like this was a dream she had never believed could become true. Daniel roared with laughter while listening to the twins' stories. Apparently they were as funny as they were talented musicians. Maggie was dancing and made anyone she could persuade join her. Charlie was trading jibes with Jack over old war stories. Claire seemed just as renewed as Zoe had been by this gathering of the chosen, all of whom appeared to be rather fascinated by Michael. Apparently having a flesh and bone Guardian in the room was not normal. Not that Zoe ever considered Michael to be normal, but she had become quite used to his otherworldly presence. The angel appeared to be terribly uncomfortable with the lavish attention from their curious new friends.

The barn was full of light and warmth and laughter. The camaraderie they had longed for was living and breathing inside those tattered walls. Zoe was swimming in it, her mind weightless. It had been longer than she could remember since she'd had a moment free from the grief and torment she'd become accustomed to. There was talk of war and battle and their enemies, but it was not from a place of fear of their potential defeat. No, this conversation was full of the robust speech of victory. Listening to it, Zoe began to believe that victory was not such wishful thinking after all.

CHAPTER TWENTY-ONE

Claire's coat wasn't enough to keep away the bite of the crisp night air. It was the price she would pay for a couple of moments alone outside of the barn, away from the festivities with their new comrades. She rubbed her arms with gloved hands in hopes of conjuring a bit of extra warmth. Music still wafted softly into the air, occasionally drowned out by the sound of Maggie's bright cackle which made Claire giggle. Then the happiness began to droop, along with the smile on Claire's face, as she felt the heaviness descend upon her. She had fought it all night, the ache inside her ribs. No matter how hard she struggled, the thoughts kept creeping back in...*Alex*.

It wasn't her fault. She knew that. She should know it after having repeated it to herself a thousand times since the moment she saw his eyes fade to black in that cave. The itch inside her brain, the demons that were trying to get in, wanted her to blame herself. She refused to let them win. She learned a long time ago that you can only control yourself, not others, not their choices or feelings or perceptions. The itchy voices would come back and admit to her that, while that was all true, she hadn't helped things. They told her that if she had really loved him, she would have let him down easy. Then this wouldn't have happened. They told her that even though it had been his choice, she had driven him to it. There was the tiniest speck of truth behind their scratchy words, just enough to make her doubt herself.

"*No!*" she screamed back at the phantom voices. She had never meant to hurt him, never meant to break his heart. A broken heart didn't turn someone into a monster.

But the scratching and itching of the shadows whispered to her, "*Your love could have saved him.*" *Could it have?*

"We do not do the saving." Michael's voice interrupted her internal dialogue. She could feel him standing behind her, the warmth emanating from him blocking the wintery chill.

"How do you do that? Know what's inside my head?" she asked, wiping at the tears that were freezing on her cheek.

Michael rested his hands on her shoulders. "I believe after all the time we have spent together, I simply know *you* that well," he replied.

Claire turned enough to see the Guardian's face. There was no visible smile, but it was still there behind his blue eyes. Knowing that she was probably the only one who was able to interpret the subtlety of his inhuman emotions caused something to stir within her, a flutter in her stomach that made her smile. She sighed, her focus returning to the starlit field. "I can't stop thinking that if I had just done something differently, if I had made myself love him again, if…"

Michael's hand slid from her shoulder, down the length of her arm until their fingers met and intertwined. "Alex chose the easy way out," he said.

"I don't think it was easy," she said.

"Seeking power is easy because the proselytes have been groomed to never fully trust love. That is how the Destroyer works. If he cannot get you to believe in a false love, a shallow, physical thing, then he promises power so that the supposed 'weakness' of love can no longer break you. But he is the broken thing. He forgot love long ago, lost it, with no hope of it being found again. He cannot understand love, and he fears it because, in its truest form, love is so much more powerful than he. The Destroyer hates love and would have found a way to twist Alex against it as long as Alex remained indentured to him. It was Alex's choice alone, and it was not about you. It was about the promise of power. Alex's own fear brought him to this end, and even your love would not have been formidable enough against that. "

Claire breathed Michael's words in deeply. He was right. Alex had been afraid, and her assurances would never have been enough because Abaddon had already gotten a grip on him. Alex had been entrapped before he'd ever resurrected on her doorstep. She squeezed the Guardian's hand. "Thank you."

"You are always welcome."

"You know, the last time we stood out here like this, you left."

"I am not going anywhere."

The flutter in her heart resumed as the tension in her shoulders relaxed. Claire leaned against Michael and watched the night sky. The itching of the shadows in her head ceased.

CHAPTER TWENTY-TWO

It was well after midnight when Zoe fell into bed and covered herself with soft blankets. She snuggled deep into their warmth. The twins' guitar tune was still playing in her head, and she let it break out into a quiet hum. She felt her eyes closing, not in the painful squeeze of fear, but with peaceful softness.

Zoe opened her eyes. The landscape was gray and red and burning. Guitars still played in the distance but their tune was slower, with minor chords, building the melody of a more tragic song. It sounded as if the strings were breaking.

"Of course you would show up tonight," Zoe said, scanning the same burning field she had stood in many times before as she'd slept. The stench and hisses and groans had grown so familiar, she was becoming numb to them.

Abaddon wasn't the large beast this time; he was now wearing the face of Mr. Achan. His shiny black shoes stepped over ashen bodies on his way to Zoe. "I couldn't resist. Now we can put some new faces on these corpses. How fabulous."

"You've overdone that bit. It doesn't have the same effect on me anymore." Zoe crossed her arms over her chest. "You should really get some new material."

"I like you like this, posing, all strong and unafraid, so much like your aunt. It's really too bad you'll never have the chance to truly mature into the woman that she is." The Destroyer paused as if in thought, a sick grin spreading over his face. He tapped his bottom lip. "I really should spend more time in her dreams."

Zoe laughed. "I don't think it would turn out the way you want. But you go ahead."

Abaddon stepped in even closer to Zoe. "Yes, I like you like this," he said again. "Your confidence will only make the stench of your fear all the sweeter." He circled around her, stopping at her back and leaning over her shoulder, his hands resting on her arms. "You want new material, how about this?"

The smoldering field morphed into the main street of town. It was dark, not because it was night, but because a black cloud had formed, circling above the crumbling buildings. It was a mixture of smoke and shadows. Zoe choked on the harsh, sickening odor of brimstone. Weeping and muffled sobs filled her ears. There was a scream from the left. "What is this?" she asked.

"This is the end," Abaddon whispered in her ear.

"Zoe!" It was Claire. She was lying on the courthouse steps. Her clothes were bloody, and she could barely sit up. Michael was lying beside her, his blue light flickering out.

"No!" Daniel yelled from across the street. Demons pulled him, their claws ripping through his flesh as they dragged him past Maggie and the creature that was feeding off her as she whimpered. Blood dripped from her mouth.

Zoe tried to take a step, but Abaddon held her in place. His tight grip was hurting her arm. "Don't look away yet," he hissed, "we are just getting to the good part."

It felt like the tears were moving up from her heart and burning in her throat like vomit. She coughed hard, and they spilled down her cheeks. She pulled against him again but couldn't break free.

Then she gasped. At the end of the street, the glint of a gold sword caught her eye. It was her, another her. She was standing in front of the Beast. He was smiling.

"I want this all to stop," she heard the other Zoe whimper.

"*This* is just beginning, but you can stop your pain, and theirs." The hellhounds on either side of the Beast howled.

The other Zoe nodded. Her drooping arms were dripping with blood. She raised the Eden sword, high and trembling. She lifted her head, and her eyes went white as the light started to appear. First, it illuminated her veins, and then her skin. Just as her whole body began to brighten, the Destroyer grabbed her by her throat. A dark stream tainted the light, and it swirled to black. Her eyes turned to fire. She screamed. The ground shook, and it was as if the sky had ripped open behind the Beast. All manner of demons began to crawl out until their darkness blotted out any trace of light in the sky.

"No," Zoe gasped again. Her body went limp. Her stomach churned.

Abaddon leaned in close, the cold skin of his cheek burned against hers. "This is how it all ends, Zoe. It doesn't matter how many people stand behind you, they will all fall because you will fall. You may be the Daughter, but you are no savior." He sniffed in deep. "Ahhh, there's the fear."

* * *

Zoe jerked awake, her arm and cheek still stinging. Her head was hurting and her nose was still burning from the smell. She sat up and glanced to the corner of her room. The Eden Sword was still leaning against the wall where she had left it, as though it was an ordinary thing, not something holy and sacred. She knew it was safe from the darkness, as their anointed home was safe, even if her mind wasn't. Watching it there, moonlight glinting off its golden edges, her nightmare flashed, and her mind saw the sword painted with her own blood. She wanted to bury it, to return it, to never have seen it. Her stomach lurched and she hurried off the bed, falling to her hands and knees as she dry heaved. When the shuddering of her empty stomach finally ceased, she pulled her weak body up and practically fell back into her bed. She pulled her knees into her thumping chest and buried her face in her pillow to stifle her sobs. *I can't do this.*

* * *

Zoe, tired and nauseated, sat tapping her spoon against the edge of her cereal bowl when Claire came down the stairs.

"Good morning," Claire lilted as she pushed the brew button on the coffee pot.

Zoe moaned a vague response. She could feel Claire staring at her from across the kitchen counter.

"You are not okay," Claire said.

"I haven't been okay for a while." A beat of panic hit Zoe's chest. She was shocked by her own honesty. She had never been so blunt about this internal battle she had been fighting. This morning she was too exhausted to hide her struggle with superficial excuses. She put her spoon down and waited for Claire's dramatic reaction.

Claire was far from dramatic. She pursed her lips, sucked air in and blew it back out. "I know," she said, reaching for her mug on the shelf.

"You know?" Zoe asked, stunned that Claire wasn't surprised.

"One, you're not a good liar. And two, I'm not a naive idiot." Claire poured half and half into her cup.

Watching her aunt act so calm, Zoe could feel the heat rise to her cheeks. "No words of wisdom? No, 'Life is hard, so suck it up kid'? Nothing?" Why was she getting angry? She didn't want a lecture, but she wanted *something* from her aunt. That was Claire's job—to make her feel better, to tell her things would be okay, to give her some perfect insight that would carry her through.

"Sorry, kiddo. I've told you everything I can think of to help you fight this. I don't have anything else."

"So that's it? It's all about the simple, 'Just take charge of your thoughts, make it go away, don't give it a foothold,' blah, blah, blah? It's not easy, you know. It keeps getting harder." Zoe's anger spilled over the walls she'd built to keep her emotions in check. She was no more in control of the bite in her words than she was of the heat that had risen to her face or the broken rhythm of her respiration.

Claire touched her hand. "Trust me, I know it's not easy. I never said it was. I can carry a sword and slay whatever demons come near you. Heck, I would march right into Hell if I thought it would fix all of this for you. But I can't help you with the war happening inside your mind, Zo. I wish I could. I wish I could climb into your dreams and fight him for you. But I can't."

Zoe's indignation transformed into hot tears that poured down her cheeks. She hated this kind of crying—the ugly cry where you lost all control and you couldn't breathe and your nose ran. She hated the sound of it and the feel of it. But hating it didn't stop it. The sobs shook her already tired body from having cried throughout most of the night.

Claire came around the counter and wrapped her arms tightly around Zoe.

Zoe locked her own arms around her aunt, clinging to her like she had done the day she woke up in the hospital after her parents died. There was a sort of release in it, the weeping. It was cleansing, like washing poison from her body. But it never completely dissipated. There was always a residue on her soul, a thin layer that would grow back to full force whenever Abaddon attacked. She would beat it back, only for it to return even more robust. With every new proliferation, the fighting became more exhausting. She was afraid, and she was tired, and she couldn't pull herself together, not this morning.

Claire just squeezed her tighter, her own tears wetting Zoe's hair. "I'm sorry it's not me," she whispered.

CHAPTER TWENTY-THREE

Zoe sat on the bottom step, waiting for Daniel to come down from his loft.

She heard the stairs creak, and then he was there, right in front of her, offering her a hand up. "You look like cr—"

"Watch it," she grumbled.

He kissed her cheek. "I think you're pretty. That was all I was going to say. You are so pretty."

Zoe rolled her eyes, then kissed his lips sweetly. "Nice save."

"Thanks." He took her hand and kissed it before pulling it to his chest, pulling her a little closer with it. "But, you know you can talk to me, right? None of us expect you to grin and bear it all alone. We know this is hard, especially on you."

"I know." She rested her head on his chest, needing his hug. "Letting everyone in is hard. When I try, it feels like I just make things worse."

"Worse? How? By being human?" he asked.

"By being selfish," Zoe replied. "I'm the Daughter. I'm supposed to save the world."

She felt his arms tighten around her and his cheek rest on her head. "Maybe we're supposed to save you," he said.

"That's a really good response," Zoe said, smiling.

"I thought so too." He chuckled then kissed her head. "Come on, let's get to the mat. I think right now Claire is the one who needs saving."

They walked hand in hand to the center of the barn. Claire was rubbing her forehead while Maggie was rambling on about something.

"What are we missing?" Zoe said, yawning.

"You look like crap." Maggie's nose wrinkled as she spoke.

Zoe crinkled her brow. "Thanks, friend."

"I care, and you can tell me all about it later. Promise. But back to me," Maggie said, crossing her arms over her chest and tapping her foot rather aggressively. "I think I should have a sword, and Claire is not in agreement."

Zoe turned to Claire. Her aunt ran her hand through her hair before responding. "I just think that a sword might..."

"Be a huge mistake," Daniel said, laughing. "But we can go back to the consecrated butter knife discussion."

Maggie stuck her tongue out at Daniel. "Laugh, go ahead," Maggie said, "but I'm serious, and I will not be deterred."

"Mags." Zoe put her hand on her friend's shoulder. "I thought the crossbow was working out. You're getting good at it and it keeps you at a safe distance."

Maggie pulled away. Zoe could see her determination as she squared her shoulders. "I'm not going to just sit on the sidelines, at a safe distance, while you all put your lives on the line," she argued. "This is just as important to me as it is to you, and I want to fight. Really fight. I can do more than be back up, or the look out, or adorable comic relief."

"Maggie, it's dangerous," Zoe pleaded.

"I know. But I'm a big girl, so teach me how to use a sword and let me fight beside you." Maggie's puppy eyes and pouty face shifted from Zoe to Claire and back again.

Claire sighed. "I'll teach you," she relented, "but whether or not you get to fight beside anyone will depend on how well you do. Got it?"

"Deal!" Maggie let out a squeal. "This is going to be awesome. And I'm totally going to take it seriously. I mean, I might be really good at this. This whole chosen thing started with three old guys in the desert, but it could end with three girls. It's symmetry, or full circle or whatever...it's cool."

Zoe echoed her aunt's chuckle before both women wrapped Maggie into a group hug.

"Uh, and what am I?" Daniel chimed in from behind them.

"Sorry," Maggie replied, "but you ruin the math. *You* can be the adorable comic relief."

Zoe peeked out from the group hug and was amused by Daniel's flustered expression. "You are adorable," she said and then winked at him. .

He smirked. "That's true, I am."

* * *

Zoe sat on the sidelines watching Maggie, who had just taken a quick break from sparring. Maggie wiped her forehead and then took a long drink from her water bottle. "Sword fighting is hard," she said.

"It gets even harder when the things you're fighting are actually trying to kill you," Daniel teased.

Maggie paused her chugging and wiped her mouth with the back of her hand. "Claire *was* trying to kill me."

"Sorry doll, Claire was going easy on you. Like, really easy." Zoe tried not to laugh at Maggie's shock. "Don't worry though, I felt the same way the first time I sparred with her. And really, I think fighting demons is easier than sparring with Claire, so you're doing good." She patted her friend's arm. Maggie wasn't as light on her feet as Zoe had been. She stumbled a few times at the beginning, but once she found her balance, she had done rather well. Zoe was proud of her. Going head to head with the Armor-Bearer was not easy; both she and Daniel could attest to that. Maggie had held her own though, and she hadn't backed down. She had surprised them.

Zoe wished she were more like her friend. Maggie had fully transformed. The trembling, insecure girl who couldn't look anyone in the eye was suddenly bright and tenacious. She was full of a joy that helped her defeat all her fears and made her so brave. Zoe envied her. She seemed light, like no burden was weighing on her, not even her sadness. It was there; Zoe knew the grief would strike Maggie whenever she thought of Lucas—whenever she missed him—but it was unlike Zoe's grief. Maggie had this way of walking around in it and not losing herself. How? How did she do it? How did she see the things she had seen; how did she lose someone she loved; how did she know the dangerous game they were all playing—and not drown?

"You still in there?" Maggie asked, waving her hand in front of Zoe's face.

Zoe shook herself. "Yeah, I'm still here, just thinking about something."

"Something good?" Maggie asked, rubbing sore muscles. Even though sweat stained her T-shirt and her hair was a mess, she still sounded chipper.

"How do you stay so, well, you?" Zoe asked her.

Maggie's head tilted to the side, and her eyes drifted upward as if she might find the answer floating above her. "I don't know," she said, shrugging. "I guess I just try not to get weighed down by the moment or the day. The end will make whatever we are going through worth it. And I remember that I'm not alone. I'm not fighting the fear, or grief, or any of it alone."

"And that works?"

"Usually, but lollipops and pie help too," Maggie answered.

Zoe laughed, thinking maybe she should keep an emergency lollipop on her at all times like Maggie.

"Time for patrol," Claire called out to them.

Zoe got up and saw that Charlie and the other descendants were all gathered at the barn doors.

"We all just gonna march down the streets together like a posse?" Daniel asked, tucking his knives into the secret pockets inside his jacket.

"No," Charlie said as he checked his weapons. "Daniel and Maggie will stick with me and Claire. We'll take Main Street all the way to the high school. Levi and the twins will drive the perimeter. Thomas, Catherine, and the Walkers will fan out near the park and the housing development. Let's all circle in and meet back here in a couple hours. Don't hesitate to call if you run into trouble. Shadows have been getting thick around here."

"What about me?" Zoe said, pulling her gloves out of her jacket pockets, ready to join the group.

The flap of wings echoed in the rafters. "You are with me," Michael said. Zoe looked over her shoulder to see him standing on the mat, his sword in hand.

"You're training with the big guy tonight. Consider it a promotion," Claire said then hugged Zoe and waved to Michael. "Have fun."

"Who says posse anymore anyway?" Charlie muttered to Daniel as the two walked past Zoe on their way outside.

The sound of car doors slamming and tires moving across the gravel let Zoe know this wasn't a prank. They had left her here, alone, with the Guardian, who was still just waiting, motionless.

"Fine," Zoe grumbled to herself. She took her jacket and winter hat back off. The Eden sword was leaning on the chair, still seeming more ordinary than it should. She stared at it for a moment, reluctant to pick it up. She still wanted to forget about it, to forget about what it meant, or what it might mean.

"It is not going to move itself," Michael said gently.

Zoe groaned, picked up the sword, and joined the angel on the gray flooring. "Okay, I'm ready."

"We will see," said the stoic Guardian.

CHAPTER TWENTY-FOUR

They had been out long enough that Claire knew everyone was miserably cold.

"I can't feel my face." Maggie pushed on her cheeks with the tips of her red fingers, which were poking through her blue gloves. "We haven't seen anything all night. Well, there was that one demon, but Claire killed it easy peasy," she said.

"It was three demons," Daniel corrected.

"Whatever. The point is, it seems to be quiet—so can we speed this thing up and go home? I can't be cold anymore. I just can't," Maggie whined.

"Unfortunately, *seems* quiet and *is* quiet are two different animals in this line of work." Claire kept her eyes moving, working to catch the slightest movement as they walked down the street. After dispatching those shadows, she had kept her sword in hand, holding it close to her side, the darkness concealing its black blade from the occasional passerby. She was not usually so bold, but she wanted to be ready; she needed to be ready.

"You sensing something?" Charlie whispered from beside her.

"Something just doesn't feel right. The cold, the quiet—it's unnatural." Claire wrapped her fingers tighter around the grip of her blade. Every sense was on alert, waiting for the tiniest hint of what was coming, because she was sure something was coming. The Destroyer had been working overtime to keep them weak and second-guessing themselves. He had to know the others had arrived into town. More demons were slipping through the veil every day. There was no way her patrol was going to be able to stroll through Torch Creek with just that one little engagement. The lights glowing over the high school parking lot came into view.

"This is our last stop." Daniel sounded more anxious now. The street lamps flickered above them as the ground trembled slightly with a barely noticeable vibration. "I think you were right," he said.

Claire stepped slowly closer to the brick building. A few cars were still scattered around the parking lot. "Why is anyone even here this late at night, over break?" she asked.

"The theater department likes to use this time to start on the sets and rehearsals for the March musical," Maggie replied.

Charlie pulled his phone from his pocket. "I'm thinking I should call for backup," he said.

There was a hiss. Claire spun toward the building. "That'd be a good idea."

Shadows were standing on the roof. It was difficult for Claire to tell how many there were, but it was no small band. Their red eyes glared fiercely at them and then they suddenly turned toward the cause of the quaking ground. So did Claire. A praetor, his rock form a towering silhouette blocking the stars, joined the demons. He roared a command and the shadows shrieked their response, and then sank inside the school.

"We need to get inside and get everyone else out," Claire ordered and took off running toward the doors with the others close on her heels.

"Do we think pulling the fire alarm will work again?" Maggie called from behind. "Because I'm game."

"We don't need police and fire trucks showing up again. We

won't be able to distract them a second time without it looking fishy," Daniel replied as he stepped into the dark entryway of the school.

"Maybe a power outage?" Charlie asked from behind. He sounded a little out of breath as he struggled to keep up with them. "The twins are pulling in. I can have them take out all power to the building. They can't rehearse if they can't see."

"Do it," Claire ordered over her shoulder as she began her slow trek down the dark hallway. She could hear voices coming from the auditorium, echoing faintly toward them, accompanied by the unmistakable sound of hissing.

They reached the closest auditorium doors and peered inside. A handful of students were delivering lines on the stage while a teacher directed them from the front row. A couple others were painting part of the set. Shadows crept around them all, black attendants in the wings and hanging from the riggings.

Claire shook her head as she watched the waiting demons. "They aren't going to get out before they get attacked. Not with those demons so close. When the lights go out, the demons will pounce."

"Well," Charlie replied coming up behind them, "time for a little acting myself." The old man tucked his machete back inside the fold of his jacket, adjusted his hat, and walked right into the theater. "Excuse me," he said, interrupting the performance, "but I think you all ought to be heading home now."

Claire watched from the door as the woman in the front row turned around with a shocked expression. "Who are you?" she asked Charlie.

"I'm the new janitor," Charlie replied. "I was here, uh, deep cleaning some classroom floors when I got the alert. Seems like some sort of storm might be coming in. You all should probably cut your rehearsal short so that you can get home safe."

"I didn't hear anything about a storm," the teacher said pulling out her smart phone.

The lights flickered but didn't go out. Claire wondered if the shadows were the cause. Then she noticed Maggie standing with her hand on the switches just inside the door.

"What? I'm helping sell this story," she said in a hurried whisper.

"See," Charlie said to the teacher. "Winds must be picking up. Power could go out any minute. You all should grab your things and call it a night."

The woman pushed her glasses up on her nose, still not appearing very convinced. So Claire nodded to Maggie who flickered the lights again, and it was enough to push her to the side of caution. "Fine. We were almost done anyway," the teacher said to Charlie. Then to the students, "Go ahead and grab your things, kids, and get home while it's safe."

"Yeah, while it's safe," Charlie repeated, tipping the bill of his hat at the teacher as she led the students up the aisle and out the opposite doors into to the main hall.

Suddenly, the electricity went off. Claire assumed the twins had arrived and cut it like Charlie had instructed. One of the students shrieked in surprise from somewhere in the hallway. Claire heard the teacher reassure her that it was just a blackout, and then told them all to have a good night. Another more chilling shriek pierced the darkness. Claire watched as red eyes blinked and shadows crept from their hiding places. The emergency lights over the exits were just enough to outline their ragged bodies.

Claire heard a commotion and turned to see Levi, Billy, and Bobby entering the auditorium from the doors the students had just exited. "Did we miss the fun?" asked Levi. Their swords were already in their hands.

"Nope. It's just getting started," Claire answered as the floor began to shake with what could only be the footfalls of a praetor. It sounded as if it were coming from behind the stage. "Maggie, take a position in the seats—wherever you can get clean shots off," she commanded. "Everyone else—let's take the stage."

Claire tried to keep one eye on her troops. She saw Charlie retrieve his machete and hack away at the two shadows that had lunged toward him. Daniel and the twins were running beside her down the aisle toward the stage. The shadows were charging, their spindly claws scratching against the concrete floor. One of Maggie's arrows whizzed by Claire, finding its home in a demon's smoky chest. She saw another arrow fly over the seats and hit the shoulder of a shadow poised behind Bobby. It shrieked and Billy finished it off for his brother. It was becoming harder and harder to keep track of the others while she cut through the shadows that were surrounding her. When one would fall, another would be there to take its place before she could catch her breath, a seemingly never-ending stream of demons.

"You all look busy," Thomas yelled from the back doors. Claire glanced up long enough to catch him jogging toward the front of the theater. Catherine, Jack, and Sue were close behind him, and all immediately joined the battle.

"You all have impeccable timing," Claire yelled as she returned her full focus to slicing through the creature in front of her.

The ground shook again. The praetor made its appearance at center stage. It had to be at least twice as tall as any man there. Its limbs were thick, its skin hard stone. It roared, the sound coarse and deep, and its eyes glowed like hot coals. The other demons seemed to grow more confident in its presence. They intensified their attacks.

"So, that's what one looks like," Daniel said from Claire's left.

"How do we kill it? Should I shoot it?" Maggie yelled from her perch.

Claire quickly glanced her way. "Do not shoot it Maggie! Those arrows aren't going to do much more than make it angry."

"Is this where we say, 'You won't like it when it's angry?'" Billy laughed from the other aisle.

"It's funny because it's true," Bobby stabbed the demon in front of him.

Claire flipped her sword around backward and drove it into the demon behind her. "You all keep working on the minions. I've got the big guy."

She ran to the stage, jumped up over the edge, and slid toward the monster. She sliced the back of its heel, then turned and pushed her blade into its other leg, right behind the joint. The creature faltered, then fell onto one knee. It thrashed its arms out, reaching for Claire. As she ducked the attack, she lifted her weapon and cut into the praetor's wrist. It roared again. Claire stepped forward, pushed off, and leaped onto the beast's back. She wrapped her arm around its wide neck and plunged her sword into its skull. The flame in the praetor's eyes dwindled as it fell forward. The Armor-Bearer hopped from its back before the monster hit the ground, its granite body cracking and breaking into hundreds of pieces, which dissolved into a pile of smoldering ash before fizzling into nothing.

Claire panted heavily. She twisted her sword in her hand, ready to hop back into the fray below her. It wasn't necessary. The shadows were gone, slain by the soldiers who now stood frozen in place, watching her in wide-eyed amazement. Claire swallowed. Adrenaline had increased her heart rate and was staving off the pain she knew would soon flood back in.

"I would not have believed it if I hadn't seen it for myself," Levi said, shaking his head slowly.

Claire hopped down from the stage near Charlie. She winced, the muscles absorbing the force of that small movement already beginning to burn.

Charlie stepped closer, taking her hands in his and turning them so he could see the inside of her arms. "You okay?"

Claire examined herself. Her jacket and shirt were singed, the skin underneath already red and forming tiny blisters. "I'll be fine. That's the secret to killing a praetor—not being afraid to get burned."

"So you *have* done that before?" Sue asked her softly as they all gathered at the front of the theater.

Claire tried to smile but the stinging of her charred skin kept her from fully succeeding. "Once or twice."

CHAPTER TWENTY-FIVE

"Again," Michael commanded.

Zoe adjusted her shirt, pulling it away from her sweaty skin. She blew a loose strand of hair off her face, and then raised her sword, stepped forward, and lunged. Michael met the move, and their swords clanked together. She spun and advanced again. Again, he blocked her. She kept pushing forward, trying her attack from every angle. He always blocked her efforts. It had been over an hour of this same dance.

"What is the point of this? You aren't even teaching me anything." Her words were separated by her wheezing. "My skill at swordplay won't matter if I can't figure out how this thing works." She swung her sword down hard.

Michael grabbed her wrist gently, stopping her sword. He stepped back slightly, letting her go and lowering his own sword. "There is no secret to the sword's power. It has no power. It merely harnesses what is already inside you," he explained.

"And how does exhausting myself by training with you help me figure out how to do that?"

"Training with me is not why you are exhausted," he replied.

"Oh, but it is."

"Zoe." Michael's voice fell somewhere between concern and correction. "Focusing the power inside you means focusing your mind. You are tired because your thoughts are moving in too many different directions. Your emotions are clouding things. You must gain control."

"You sound like Claire," Zoe huffed.

"Perhaps Claire sounds like me. She had to learn this same lesson—to take charge of her worries, her fears, her anger." He drew out that last word.

"I'm not angry." Zoe squeezed her sword's grip and retreated from the mat to retrieve her water bottle.

"You are," Michael replied, soft but unmoving. Zoe thought she heard him sigh. "The Eden sword may not hold power itself, but it is special. It was forged in the sacred spaces of heaven. It is not of this earth and cannot function as though it is. It must be wielded with sacred intentions, not earthly ones."

"I have no idea what any of that means," Zoe said.

"It means you must find your way beyond your grief and anger. If you don't, then either fear will stop you, or you will charge forward only for revenge, and your power cannot function tainted by that darkness." Michael's voice had sharpened. It couldn't be categorized as angry, or even frustrated, but she knew he was challenging her, pushing her.

Zoe turned back to the stoic angel, still in the spot where she had left him on the mat. "What do you suggest I do about it then? Fake it 'til I make it? Forget about Lucas? Become some robot, a tin man with no heart?" She *was* angry. It was coming out again, and it startled her. She had been so good at hiding it deep inside and covering it with sadness that she hadn't known so much anger was even there. But now that it had been revealed, it wouldn't submit to her attempts to recover it.

Michael's eyes seemed to grow brighter. His broad shoulders moved up and down with the intake of a silent sigh. "Find forgiveness, Zoe."

A laugh erupted out of Zoe's throat, a scoff at the Guardian's suggestion. "Forgive the devil? Sure, no problem." She laughed again.

"He is not the one you need to forgive."

CHAPTER TWENTY-SIX

"You sure you're okay?" Claire asked Zoe who was sitting on the edge of her bed, brushing her wet hair.

"Are you?" Zoe shot right back at her with a lifted eyebrow.

"How about we both just get some sleep," Claire relented. "Goodnight, Zo." She yawned.

"Night."

Claire yawned again. She was exhausted from the night's brawl. Her muscles ached. The hot bath she had taken earlier did little to curb the painful effects of battle. She was thankful Michael had healed the wound on her arm. She would never have been able to sleep through the irritation of the burn, and she needed to sleep. Her body and her soul needed rest. A soft bed and warm blankets would be a welcome end to this day.

* * *

Claire could feel the flakes tickling her face before she opened her eyes to the wintry forest. It was a beautiful scene. The dark evergreen branches were frosted white. The tall trees grew from beneath a pure blanket of fresh snow. It was clean and quiet. It would have been a peaceful dreamscape, walking through those woods. But Claire knew better. She didn't need the familiarity of demons filling her senses to know her enemy was stalking her. With a single thought, a sword appeared in her hand, forming as if out of the cold air.

"Tisk, tisk," said Meredith as she approached from between the trees, snow crunching under her black boots. "Here I am just wanting to chat about your day, and you go and bring a weapon. That's not very nice."

"Sorry, but I know how our little chats usually end," Claire responded. Her muscles immediately tensed, and her nerves tingled under her skin as they went on the alert. "What do you want?" she asked.

"I told you, I wanted to chat. You know, girl talk?" Meredith leaned against one of the nearby tree trunks.

"Want to braid each other's hair and paint our toenails too?" Claire asked, squeezing the grip of her sword. She was losing patience with whatever trick Meredith was playing.

"Have you always been this funny?" Meredith gibed. "I was thinking we could talk about boys, one or two in particular." Meredith's smile was lined with cruelty.

The itchy thoughts had started scratching inside Claire's mind again. She could hear them shouting their arguments, trying to break her down. She wouldn't let them, not here in front of her enemy. She concentrated on another voice—Michael's. It was just a whisper, and though the demon voices were trying to drown it out, the more she zeroed in on it, the louder it became. *We do not do the saving.* His words became louder, driving the tormenting notions away.

"I'm not really in the mood to hear about your warped love life," Claire said with a sigh. "Maybe another time."

"Oh, I don't want to talk about *my* love life. I want to talk about yours and how truly pathetic it is." Meredith played with a strand of her black hair, twisting it between two fingers. "You love an angel that you know you can't be with, and who probably doesn't love you in return anyway. I mean, all these years with you were just his duty, and the moment he got called away, he didn't hesitate to leave you all alone."

"What you're doing won't work," Claire said, trying to stay focused on the truths she knew so that Meredith's lies couldn't gain the high ground in her mind.

Meredith pushed away from the tree she had been leaning against and began to creep closer to Claire. "And what about Alex?" she asked. "Let's not even get into the part about you driving him away, breaking his heart. He was supposed to be your happily-ever-after. He could have been, you know. He could've been your ticket away from all this. But you killed him."

"I didn't kill him." Claire bit out the words in a steely whisper.

"Semantics," Meredith declared and snapped her fingers.

Demons shrieked behind Claire. She saw a trail of blood staining the white snow. Her chest tightened as she followed the crimson traces deeper into the wood. The trees seemed to hiss as she stepped past them, demons hiding in their branches but yet unseen. There was a small clearing ahead of her. A writhing figure lay on the ground. The falling snow sprinkled over the bloody clothes as demons tore into the flesh.

"Claire," the dying figure coughed out between screams

"Alex!" Claire gasped in recognition. She ran toward him.

She felt the tears begin to cascade down her cheeks, and she had just about reached Alex when his screaming turned to laughter. She halted as he stood up, wiping a trickle of blood from his curved lips.

"Don't pretend this upsets you—that you care," he said, dismissing her tears.

"I cared. I do care." Claire's chest tightened, holding her cracked heart together.

"If you cared, I wouldn't be like this." Alex's eyes turned black, and the demons that had been part of his charade slinked to his side.

"You were *this* from the moment you came back," Claire countered. "I have wracked my brain, thinking of what I could have done differently, but Michael was right, this isn't about me, this is about you being afraid and—"

"Of course the angel would say that," Alex said as he dusted snow off his jacket. "He would say anything to make you feel better—to make you feel—"

"He cares for me, I can't deny that," Claire said. She refused to let the itchy, torturous thoughts back into her brain. "But Michael doesn't lie. He doesn't manipulate. It isn't who he is."

"I never realized I was competing with Mr. Perfect," Alex scoffed.

"You weren't competing with anyone but yourself. You chose to shut down and shut me out. You kept me at a distance as much as I did you. Abaddon made sure of that." Claire watched the truth in her words hit Alex.

His eyes went wide and he swallowed. She saw the rhythm of his chest quicken.

Meredith stepped from the sidelines, closer to Alex. She slid her long fingers onto his shoulder. "The Destroyer saved you. He showed you the truth, that she would never love you again, that she was the one lying, like she is now."

"I'm not," Claire said staring into Alex's dark eyes. The black faltered and his normal blue was beginning to peek through.

"Please," Meredith scoffed. "You gave up on him the moment the shadows stopped his heart and stole his soul. The Destroyer was there to put him back together." Meredith drew her sword.

Claire ignored Meredith's glimmering blade. "I almost died mourning you," she pleaded with Alex. "If it hadn't been for Zoe, I would have let those demons, the ones who dragged you to Hell, rip me to pieces. September sixteenth would have been my end because I didn't want to live without you."

All darkness left Alex's eyes, replaced by glassy tears. The demons beside him hissed in displeasure.

"Enough of this!" Meredith charged.

Claire lifted her sword just in time to block the attack. She shoved Meredith backward, both of them slipping in the snow.

"You can't trust her, Alex." Meredith swung at Claire again.

"But he can trust you?" Claire asked incredulously as she dodged the strike. She sliced her blade through the air. It clashed with Meredith's, the sound echoing through the trees.

"Even if you loved him once, you don't now. What if the Guardian were here? Who would you choose?" Meredith's words were accompanied by another lunge and parry.

Claire glanced toward Alex. Her words could make the difference. If she could tell him she would choose him, he would give in, he would come back to her, but it would only be temporary. Her pretty words weren't what he needed anyway. He needed the truth. "I don't know, but being with you, Alex—it isn't even a possibility as long as Abaddon's claws are dug into your heart," she managed to say between trading blows with Meredith. "...but this can't be about me, Alex. It's about you—it's about choosing what's right. They aren't interested in your happiness. They don't care about you." Claire shoved Meredith backward causing the proselyte to slip and fall in the snow, creating enough space and time for her to turn to Alex, but it was too late.

The shadows beside Alex had slinked closer and were whispering in his ears. His face hardened and his eyes grew black again. "Neither do you," he said as he lifted his hands and more shadows climbed out of the snow, their claws digging into the cold ground as they pulled themselves up.

Claire stiffened her shoulders and hastened the pace of her sword blows. Meredith was up, charging at her again and appeared more aggressive in her assault. Claire intensified her own defense, turning from Meredith to cut down the demon at her side and back in time to block another cut from the proselyte. This same sequence repeated, beats of swordplay interrupted by the slicing of an intrusive shadow.

More and more demons circled Claire. Their ashen bodies blurred around her as she lunged and dodged. She was having a harder time keeping up with the onslaught. Claire kicked forward, her foot driving into Meredith's stomach, shoving her opponent back again. She bought herself another few seconds to devote to slaying the demons that were lashing at her.

Meredith recovered and growled, then launched herself back at Claire. She brought her arm down, crashing her elbow against Claire's face. Claire stumbled, and Meredith punched her again, then kicked her. The Armor-Bearer fell to one knee.

Anticipating the next blow, Claire rolled out of the way before getting back onto her bare feet. It was enough to elude Meredith's strike, but not enough to avoid the shadows. She felt claws digging into her back. She stifled the cry of pain and spun, slicing through the creature.

Claire felt blood soaking through her shirt. She'd had enough. This invasion had gone on too long. She had allowed it to go on too long, but she was finished. With a single thought, a second blade appeared in Claire's empty hand. She spun the two swords simultaneously.

"I've had quite enough of this," the Armor-Bearer declared, determined not to play defense any longer as she rushed toward Meredith. Her every movement was fluid, her blades swinging in arcs all around her, taking out every demon that dared to draw near. They dissolved in clouds of dust and ash that sprinkled the ground. Something primal stirred within Claire and erupted from her in a soft roar. She brought one blade up, ready to cut down the raven-haired proselyte. She pushed off the ground and leaped toward her combatant, but her sword only sliced through smoke.

Meredith had disappeared in a puff of black smog. Claire spun on her heel to find Alex and his demons gone as well. She was alone once again, but the scene was no longer pristine. The snow was littered with soot and blood. Her swords had become heavy in her hands; they drooped at her sides until she finally dropped them. Her wounds stung with every respiration. She begged herself to wake up.

* * *

"Claire." Michael's whisper broke through the curtain of sleep.

Tears were already sticking to Claire's lashes before she opened her eyes. Liquid was dripping from her nose. She lifted her finger to wipe it away. It was blood, bright red and dribbling onto her lip.

"Here," Michael said, handing her a tissue.

She took it and stuffed it against her nostril. "How did you?" she asked.

"Our souls are tethered, remember? I know when you are in distress. This time I would not simply stand by and watch." His bright blue eyes watched her, his brow was creased. "Are you all right?"

She wanted to just say yes, a simple yes, but she couldn't push the word out of her mouth. Instead she choked out a sob before answering, "He's gone—lost—to them."

Michael's strong arms wrapped around her, drawing her into the warmth of his chest. She felt his cheek against the top of her head. "No one is ever so lost that they cannot be found again," he said.

"I'm afraid he won't want to be found." She was reliving that September Tuesday, what would have been her wedding day; the day she had almost let them take her. The pain of her previous mourning flooded her heart. It was as if Alex had died all over again. It was his choosing, but that knowledge didn't help her to swallow the ache. Her misery, then and now, was more than grief; it was guilt. She should never have fallen for him; she had known that. Alex had been a deviation from the loneliness of a path she had grown tired of walking. If she had been stronger back then, stayed her course, he wouldn't have become a casualty of her war. She had been weak. She had made a mistake, and it was haunting her and destroying him.

"You have to give him over. Trust that there is another love that can rescue him still," Michael reassured her.

Tears spilled down her cheeks and onto her hands that clung to

Michael's shirt. Another sob shook her shoulders. The shudder moved inward, toward the hidden places in her spirit. The ache reached deep within until it pierced her soul. Warmth seeped from the hole the pain had made, a soothing whisper of love that was beyond her own frail renderings. Its serenity soaked through her bones and consumed her fears and failures. She would not be defeated by what she could not control, by choices which could not be undone or were not her own. *You do not do the saving, dear one.*

"Thank you," Claire whispered, her gratitude stretching beyond her Guardian to the still small voice carried on the waves of peace. She rested against the angel as the sun rose outside her window.

CHAPTER TWENTY-SEVEN

Christmas lights were still wrapped around the trees that lined Torch Creek's Main Street. Green garland with red bows still hung from the lampposts. It was warmer though, feeling more like spring than New Year's Eve. Zoe and Daniel had walked the old town thoroughfare the better part of the night, popping into the quaint shops and pausing for the occasional performance by a local artist or musician. Merriment surrounded them but it stopped short of penetrating Zoe's mood. She yearned to cast off her worries. How nice would it be to forget about the past and ignore the future for one night?

"Here I thought y'all were turning into hermits or something," a voice echoed from the back of the diner they had just entered. Zoe looked to see their classmate Anna, her red curls bouncing with each step she took toward them. "There are more seats in the back corner with us," she said, pointing at Kyle and Josh who were waving.

Zoe didn't want to sit with them. Not because she didn't like them—they were fun—but fun simply felt too uncomfortable now. She just wanted to grab a coffee and go back to wandering around the festivities quietly with Daniel. It wouldn't happen, though, because Daniel would be polite. She could see from his awkward smile that her assessment was about to be proven correct.

"Sure," Daniel said, tugging Zoe by the hand as he followed Anna back to their table.

Josh scooted further into the booth to make room for them. "What have you guys been up to?" he asked. "I feel like we never see you anymore."

"Uh…" Zoe couldn't think of what to say. Killing demons and taking names didn't seem like an appropriate response, but it was all that sprang to her mind. She grinned at Daniel as she thought about how much fun it might be to just toss the truth out there and see their reaction. Lucas would have agreed. She wouldn't do it though. Thinking of him had stolen the humor from the moment anyway.

"Not much, studying mostly," Daniel said, coming to her rescue.

"Where's Maggie?" Kyle asked, setting down his coffee. "I bet she's been bummed since that Lucas kid left. She seemed to like him."

Zoe felt the grief push further upward but managed to shove it down. She squeezed Daniel's hand and hoped her voice wouldn't tremble. "Yeah…uh…her parents have this New Year's Eve movie marathon tradition thing, so she's home."

"Oh," Kyle replied.

Did he notice her discomfort? Did he see the tears trying to force their way out?

"What have you guys been up to?" Daniel asked.

He was good at being her white knight. Zoe was quite certain she had been given a gift in Daniel. He was patient and kind and thoughtful. He treated her like he didn't deserve her, but more and more she thought she was the undeserving one. High school relationships didn't usually work out, but this didn't feel like high school. It wasn't shallow or self-serving like most other relationships at their age. Zoe reminded herself they were still getting to know each other, and while in some ways their life as descendants

had given them an intimacy which grew steadily deeper, an inno-
cence still remained. Zoe liked the feel of it, pure and slow. She
could sense it steady her in a world that often left her so off-
balance. She thought she could love Daniel forever. When she
allowed herself to dream of uncertain futures, it would be of one
with him. Practicality always pulled her from her musings though.
The corpse-field of her nightmares reminded her that a life with
him was improbable, perhaps impossible.

Zoe smiled at Daniel, snuggling a little closer to him. She
ignored the conversation around her. She wanted to focus
completely on the gift that was this moment, every moment with
him. Even if they were only for now and had no hope of lasting
beyond these temporal days, she would try to treasure every one
of them. For one brief point in time, here and now, at the end of
this year, she would not neglect this blessing.

"How about you Zoe, what did you get for Christmas?" Anna
asked, interrupting Zoe's rumination.

Again, she thought of how Lucas might have answered,
shocking their companions with tales of golden swords of destiny.
She chuckled to herself and gave the less entertaining answer. "My
Aunt Claire got me this bracelet," she said holding up her wrist.

"Cute," Anna said. She caught the dangling charm with her
fingers and mouthed the inscription as she read it. She looked at
Zoe with an open mouth, and seemed as if she were about to
comment or question further, when the barista announced the ball
drop would be starting in just a few minutes at the courthouse
steps.

Josh grabbed his jacket as he stood up. "We better go so we can
get a good view," he said.

"You two coming?" Kyle asked.

"You three go on ahead," Daniel said as he linked his fingers
with Zoe's.

"We get it—the lovebirds want to be alone," Anna said,
giggling. "Happy New Year, you two!"

"Happy New Year," Zoe replied. Her voice barely made it over the noise of the exiting patrons to elicit a small wink and wave from Anna as she stepped outside.

"Still want that coffee?" Daniel asked.

Zoe leaned close, placing a sweet kiss on his lips.

"What was that for?"

"For being you."

Daniel responded with his own soft kiss. "I'm gonna forgive how cheesy this moment is because I like you so much."

"I'm not cheesy—I'm adorable." Zoe giggled as she pulled him to his feet. "Now, let's get that coffee and go ring in the New Year."

A few minutes later Zoe was sipping her latte, still smiling, her arm linked with Daniel's while they walked toward the crowd waiting at the courthouse. They were already counting down the final seconds of the year as a glittering disco ball was slowly being lowered.

Ten...nine...

Zoe, like always, could smell it first. The ash and blood tickled her nose. She surveyed the street and swore she saw glowing eyes scattered among the spectators. When she blinked, they were all gone.

Eight...seven...

A scream echoed. She jerked her head, and an image from the nightmarish vision Abaddon had shown her replayed in her mind —Maggie lying on the curb.

Six...five...four...

Another blink and reality blurred again. She watched Daniel being dragged into the alleyway. "No," she whispered, and the specter was gone. The street was full again and she was clinging to Daniel's arm.

"You okay?" Daniel whispered.

Three...two...

Another scream distracted Zoe. She peered ahead through all the chanting and cheering partiers who slowly faded to reveal Claire lying, bleeding on the courthouse steps and Michael dying beside her.

"This isn't real."

"What isn't?" Daniel asked, grabbing Zoe's arms and maneuvering her to look him in the eye. "Zoe, what's going on?"

"He ruins everything. He's going to take everything away from me, destroy every moment of happiness." Happy-New-Years were shouted as fireworks whizzed and then boomed overhead, but none of that could subdue Zoe's fear. It trembled inside her, shaking the oxygen out of her lungs.

"Zo, Abaddon isn't here," Daniel said. His stare was intense, pushing his eyebrows tighter together. His eyes darted back and forth, as if they were searching for something in hers. His lips were parted like a word had been on the tip of his tongue, ready to spring out, but got lost.

Zoe wanted to tell him she was fine. She wanted to lie and say she was just tired. It would only be a half-lie. Half or whole, it wouldn't find its way out. Neither would the tears that she could feel, heavy things waiting behind her eyes. She blinked hoping to release them, but it didn't work. The fear rumbled again. "He's always here," she whispered.

Daniel hugged her. His cheek rested against the top of her head. "You have to fight him, Zo."

Her latte dropped to the ground spilling open. "I'm tired of fighting," Zoe said, "I'm not some soldier. I'm not a warrior."

"We are all warriors," Daniel replied. "We may not feel like it, but we are. Descendant, bloodline, prophecy—none of it matters. We all fight the darkness every day."

Zoe pulled back until she was free from his embrace. "This isn't some normal situation, some small daily tragedy. This is for the whole world, life and death," she said.

Daniel's face softened but his eyes remained fierce. "Those are always the stakes," he said. "It's always life and death. Most people are just never aware of that fact."

Zoe watched the bright colors lighting up the black canvas above them. "I want that ignorance back," she said.

"That's not going to happen," Daniel said stepping behind her, resting his hands on her shoulders. His thumbs circled against her tense muscles. "But I don't think ignorance is what you need back —I think it's faith."

"Easy for you to say. I'm the Daughter. I'm the one who has to carry the sword. I'm the one who will walk into Hell alone." She turned out of his touch to look directly at his face.

"You aren't alone. You will never be alone," he said as he took her hand.

"Faith seems like a luxury—something for people who can't see the truth. I mean, it feels like the Maker has forgotten about us— about me. He hasn't exactly been making Himself known." Her tears grew even heavier and finally began to tip over her long lashes.

"This girl I know once told me the Maker was a big enough boy to handle us being mad at Him. Maybe the problem isn't that He hasn't shown up, but that you've just stopped seeing Him." Daniel brushed his hands across her cheeks, wiping her tears away with his fingers. "Maybe you need to open your eyes."

"It's that easy?" she asked, hopeful.

A wistful smile pricked at the corners of Daniel's lips. "Or that hard," he said.

CHAPTER TWENTY-EIGHT

The sun was still new, its faint light edging out navy blue skies behind the barn. Claire slipped off her shoes at the edge of the mat. Her steps were light, silent like the space around her. She raised her sword in front of her and slid her hand down its cool, black metal. It had been a while since she had been alone with her inanimate companion. She was so familiar with it, its weight and length and history, that she had let it become a common thing. She took for granted the sacredness it held. Her sword was as old as their bloodline itself. It had slain more evil than she could fathom facing in her lifetime. It had survived centuries and would live on long after her body was dust.

Claire closed her eyes and tilted her head forward in a solemn bow. She twisted the blade in her right hand and stepped her left foot forward. She began her slow dance. The choreography wasn't about battle or even survival; it was an offering, a retreat into a holy space that she had neglected. Lyrical movements stretched her muscles and awoke the sleepy places in her heart. The wind circled around her, an invisible partner. One final turn, a lunge forward, and then with her feet together, she brought the sword down straight, its tip resting on the mat. Claire dropped to her knees and bowed forward. She hung her head low and felt her shoulders stretch with each deep breath as new life seemed to prickle over her skin.

"It has been quite some time since I last saw you in such reverence." The Guardian's deep voice echoed through the rafters.

Claire wiped her eyes. "It has been quite some time, period."

Michael reached out his hand and Claire took it, allowing him to help her stand. She was reluctant to let it go.

"Are we interrupting something?" Charlie asked, pulling Claire's attention. He scratched his head, moving his hat out of place.

"No," Claire answered. She felt heat blush across her cheeks. She leaned against Michael's arm, squeezed his hand, and then let it go. "You here for target practice?"

"Actually," said Charlie, "Levi here thinks he can outshoot me, so we're here so I can embarrass him."

"There will be humiliation but it won't be mine, old man," Levi boasted as he brushed past Charlie on his way to the archery targets.

"Who you callin' old?" Charlie asked. He grimaced, fixed his hat, and then followed Levi.

"Isn't it a little early for this amount of surly?" Claire asked as she slipped her shoes back on.

"We're not surly—"Charlie began.

"We're delightful," Levi cut him off and finished.

Claire laughed at the two men. Her phone began ringing inside her bag and it took her a minute to dig it out. "Hello," she finally answered.

She heard Zoe's voice on the other end, talking so fast about eating breakfast in town with Daniel and Maggie, and then seeing them, demons, everywhere. "They're feeding off people right out in the open!" she exclaimed.

"Don't do anything. We're coming," Claire commanded, then

clicked off the phone and shoved it into her back pocket. "We need to get the others and get into town, now."

"What's going on?" Charlie asked as he shot his arrow.

"Zoe just called," Claire replied, "demons are all over Main Street."

"A little brave aren't they? In the daylight, with the Daughter here?" Levi asked as he scratched at the scruff that covered his chin.

Charlie was tucking arrows back into the pockets that lined the inside of his jacket.

"One or two is normal but..." he said.

"Ten. Twenty. More. That sure isn't." Claire pulled her coat on and checked each of its hidden spaces for her other knives. "Get the others. Let's meet up outside the Haven."

She followed Charlie and Levi out of the barn toward the line of RVs and tents. The other descendants were already tossing on jackets and checking weapons as they stepped into the morning. Claire and Michael hopped into her SUV and took off down the driveway. She glanced in the rearview to make sure the others were following.

When they reached the Haven, Claire stopped the vehicle right in front of the building. She hurried to open her door as she cut the engine. Zoe, Daniel and Maggie were already coming out of the cafe's doors to meet them.

"What do we do?" Zoe asked, grabbing Claire's arm. "We can't exactly pull out our swords right here in front of the townsfolk."

"We have to do *something*," Daniel said and nodded across the street.

Claire followed his gaze. There was a couple arguing outside one of the small stores. On either side of them were shadows hovering above the sidewalk with their claws dug into the unwary couple's backs. The creatures' red eyes were glowing bright, and they licked black drool from their ashen lips as they seemed to puppet the pair of humans. Just down from them, another demon was following a young girl who was crying. Still another stood behind an old woman who was staring into a boutique window. Claire surveyed the rest of the street in a slow turn that ended with her peering in through the front glass doors of the Haven. Inside, she saw red eyes blinking and heard the hisses and whispers of shadows underscoring the soft music of an oldies radio station. She could also see so much pain and anger and fear written across the patrons' faces. It radiated out from them and permeated the air in a stench that burned her nostrils and sickened her stomach.

While Claire was surveying the situation, the rest of the descendants had gathered around her and Zoe.

Maggie pushed herself further inside the huddle by Zoe. "Can't you just do what you did with me, that first day?" she asked.

"I don't think awkward chit chat and pie are going to do the trick this time, Mags," Zoe replied.

"Everybody loves pie," Maggie retorted, "but that's not what I mean. I mean the truth. Like with me and like what we did at the school when Abaddon had everyone pulling the mannequin challenge."

"Last time everyone was in a trance." Zoe shook her head slowly. "It was easy to whisper in their ears and have it push through the fear. Besides, it only took one or two for Abaddon to give in and retreat."

"I don't think this is Abaddon, not specifically," Claire interrupted, but kept her eyes moving, taking note of every demon that had infiltrated the sidewalks and shops.

"You are correct," Michael said. The Guardian stood close to her. "This is the reaping. The veil continues to weaken. More demons are breaking through, and they need food so they are growing bolder. More will come and this will only get worse until they begin to spread beyond Torch Creek's borders and infect other towns." He leaned in front of Claire to address Zoe. "You can stop this," he said.

"No, I can't," Zoe responded. Her face paled and she wrapped her arms around herself, tucking her hands under. "Even if I thought I could, I don't have my sword," she stuttered.

"It's in the car," Claire said, jerking her head in that direction. Daniel walked over and retrieved the golden blade from the backseat. "You have to at least try," Claire encouraged her niece.

Zoe took the weapon from Daniel. "People will see."

"They won't," Charlie said, gesturing for everyone to circle in tighter. "The demons don't need to see the power—they'll feel it."

"What if I ..." Zoe began a question but never finished. Instead she looked at the ground.

Claire took her niece's face in her hands. Zoe was trembling. "Just try," she smiled, "and trust."

Zoe nodded and Claire released her. She watched her niece step back, bow her head and close her eyes. When they opened again they were growing milky. The light was dim but it was there. There was a gasp from the others, accenting their looks of amazement. The air grew warmer inside their circle. The white light flickered in Zoe's veins, sparking its way down her fingers toward the Eden sword.

The shadows began to screech.

"Keep going Zoe," Daniel said.

"It isn't going to be enough. I can feel it. It's too weak," Zoe whimpered. Her face was clenched and sweat was beading on her forehead. "I'm not strong enough. This is just making them angry."

Claire was watching their enemy. The demons had all trained their blazing eyes toward the cluster.

"That may be all we need for right now," Claire said. The creatures twitched as they began their slow advance. "Lead them toward the old hardware store. We can fight them there."

The huddle began moving across the street with their hands on their hidden weapons. Zoe was next to Claire, still at the center. The light in her eyes was fading faster now, but it didn't matter.

The demons were doing what they had expected them to do—slinking after them.

Claire nodded to Billy, who kicked in the wooden door of the abandoned hardware store and all the descendants ducked inside. The demons, apparently unable to ignore an opportunity to kill members of the bloodline, had picked up their pace and were closing in. The mass tried to funnel in through the same front door, but some split off and could be heard clawing at the boarded windows and scratching their way up the outer brick walls to the upper level.

"They are going to try and pin us in," Thomas said, twisting the daggers in his hands.

"Let them. They won't make it back out of this building," Claire replied, then drew her sword.

Claire knew no further direction was needed; each soldier would take their positions, weapons ready to bring destruction upon their murky enemies. The skirmish that ensued was a blur to her. Demons were screeching, and arrows were whizzing through the room. Claire could hear her comrades' heavy steps and cooperative commands.

"Watch your six!"

"Demon on your left!"

"Duck!"

The Armor-Bearer skewered the demon lunging at her, spun to trade places with Michael, and then sliced the neck of the next shadow she faced. She chanced a glance toward Zoe who was fighting beside Daniel in the corner. Maggie was behind them, reloading her crossbow. They were holding their own. She couldn't worry about them though. They could handle themselves and she needed to focus.

"Levi!" Charlie's familiar voice echoed down the stairs followed by a groan.

A demon shrieked, and then there was a loud crash that Claire assumed came from upstairs because dust rained down from the ceiling. Claire inclined an ear, trying to listen to the scuffle above her as she dispatched the final few demons around her. The others must have been having the same success with the attacking shadows because the number of enemies was quickly dwindling to nothing around her. They would be able to walk away with not much more than a few small burns or claw marks between them— except for Levi. Charlie and Jack were on either side of him at the top of the stairs, holding him up as he struggled down each step. His eyelids looked heavy, and blood was running down his chest and arm from a large wound on his neck.

"What happened?" Claire asked, meeting them at the bottom of the staircase.

"Darn thing bit him," Charlie replied. "Clawed onto his back and dug its fangs right in." Charlie cautiously took the last stair, adjusting Levi's weight on his shoulder as they reached the first floor. "Nasty bugger didn't want to let go either."

"I've had worse," Levi said, then coughed. His mouth curved into a weak smile that showed his blood-painted teeth.

"Can you?" Claire asked Michael.

Michael eyed the wound, then replied, "It is deep. I do not think I can heal it completely myself, but I can do enough to keep him alive." Michael touched the lesion. Levi's blood dribbled through his fingers, mixing with the blue glow. When the Guardian removed his hand, the bleeding had stopped, but Levi's dark skin was still broken and marred.

"Thank you," Levi muttered.

Michael dipped his head in a small bow.

"Jack, let's take him to get cleaned up and rested," Sue said, stepping up from somewhere behind her husband.

Jack nodded, and he and Charlie began to walk Levi toward the door. A slow applause reverberating from the top of the stairs stopped them.

Claire turned to see Meredith saunter halfway down, then lean against the railing. "That Guardian of yours comes in handy," she said. "Seems he's not just a pretty face."

Claire noticed Michael's blue eyes blaze brighter. She touched his arm gently, an effort to calm him, then moved toward the proselyte, positioning herself on the stairway between her raven-haired enemy and the other descendants. "You know you can't take us all on by yourself, so why are you here?" she asked.

Meredith touched her hand to her chest, feigning shock. "Can't I just stop by and say hello?"

"No," Maggie retorted.

"I like her." Meredith chuckled. "But, truly, I just came to watch the fracas, a little early morning entertainment. I must say you all were almost impressive. I'd be scared, but this was just an appetizer, you've no idea—"

"We know more demons are coming," Claire said. She squeezed the grip of her sword.

"*Here*. More demons are already here," Meredith corrected. "The only reason this town hasn't been swallowed whole is because Abaddon is using them, gathering them together to harness their energy in preparation—"

"For what, exactly?" Daniel interrupted.

"For her." Meredith pointed a slender finger at Zoe. "It's only a matter of time before this all ends bloody. He's nearly ready. Are you?" she asked, looking only at Zoe.

Claire lunged toward Meredith, but in the few seconds it took her to make the short climb, the proselyte had disappeared in a cloud of black smoke.

* * *

Claire sat on the sofa, legs crossed under a fleece blanket and a carton of sweet and sour chicken in her hands. "How's Levi?" she asked as Michael appeared in the middle of the room.

"He is resting and his wound is healing well. He will be fine."

"That's good." She picked up another bite and popped it in her mouth before it slid from the precarious grip of her chopsticks. "Want some?" Claire asked, holding her carton out to the

Guardian and then used it to gesture at several other cartons sitting open on the coffee table.

Michael looked in each before picking up the lo mein and taking a seat next to Claire. "Where are Zoe and Daniel?" he asked.

"Eating in the kitchen. I figured they could use some alone time," she explained and took another bite.

Michael nodded and then scooped up a clump of noodles. He looked very normal, very human. The whole moment was weird in so much as it wasn't. They were used to shadows and battle and prophecies ruling their time together, but right now there were none of those things. There were no demons hiding in corners, no need to talk of journals and weapons and war. They were just two people like any others, sitting together, eating dinner in blissful peace. *Is this what it could be like?* Claire wondered.

"Are you all right?" Michael was staring at her over his food.

"Actually, I feel better than I have in a very long time," she admitted. "I know I should probably be worried about something, panicking over what we should do next, but I'm not." She traded out her carton for a different one and poked at some fried rice.

"Perhaps your faith in the Way has been renewed," Michael said just before he took another bite.

"I guess it's about time." Claire giggled as Michael slurped up a long noodle. "I just needed to regain my focus. Too much was pulling at me, distracting me from... I don't know, reality, the truth..."

"Distractions like Alex?" Michael asked.

Claire stirred through the rice, pushing aside the bits of onion she didn't like, thinking how much easier it would be if she could only pick out the unwanted bits of life that easily. "My heart still hurts for him," she confessed.

Michael touched her knee. "You would not be you if it did not," he said.

"Alex was good. He was charming, sweet, thoughtful..." An image of him flickered in her memory, his smile when they first met. It made Claire's stomach flutter and ache all at the same time.

"I regret the way things happened between us. I regret my fear. I regret losing myself in it." More memories intruded. Their first kiss and their last. His screams. Her mourning, and the shadows that almost took her. "That's not what love is supposed to be...you shouldn't get lost. You should be more of who you are. The Armor-Bearer is who I am, and Alex never knew her, and that means I probably never really knew him."

"But you did love him," Michael stated.

She touched Michael's hand that still lingered on her knee. "Yes, I did. I still do. Not in the way I had believed back then, but enough to wish better for him now."

"He must wish it for himself."

"I know," Claire said, returning her attention from the angel's piercing eyes back to her lukewarm dinner. "I still wish I had learned some of these lessons back then. But maybe the timing is just as important as the learning." She shoveled in a bite of rice.

Michael sighed. "I wish I had done things differently myself."

It wasn't the words but the sadness that made her stop chewing and hold her breath, waiting for what he might say next.

"I should not have left you, Claire." The Guardian's jaw was clenched, his eyes glassy.

Claire took Michael's carton from his hands and set it on the table next to hers. She turned her whole body to better face him and gently took both of his hands in her own. "I used to be angry that you did," she said, squeezing his hands even tighter. "What happened after you left was my fault—my mistake. I forgot it wasn't about you, and it wasn't about me. But you were right. Daniel needed you. If you hadn't obeyed, then he wouldn't be here, and I am so glad he is here. Zoe needs him." She moved one hand to touch his face gently. "She needs him as much as I need you."

Michael leaned against her touch, wrapping his fingers around her petite wrist. "I will not leave you again," he whispered.

"Good."

Claire scooted closer, sidling against her Guardian. She rested her head on his shoulder. He wrapped his arm around her. She loved him. Whether anything normal was a possibility for them or not, she would no longer deny that longing. She wouldn't pursue it, but she wouldn't silence it either. She didn't need romance. She didn't need a fairytale ending. She needed him, beside her. If all he could ever be was the man sitting next to her and nothing more— that would be enough.

CHAPTER TWENTY-NINE

Zoe moved her food around on her plate with her fork, having abandoned her chopsticks after her futile attempts at using them had failed.

"Not hungry?" Daniel asked as he refilled his plate with another helping of rice. "You need to eat, Zo."

"I know," she said, then let out a quiet sigh. Food wasn't all Zoe needed. She needed sleep. She needed focus. She needed courage. She needed air because she felt like she was drowning. She knew the rest of the world probably just saw a young girl sitting at a scratched and worn dining table covered in way too much takeout. Perhaps, if the world were observant enough, they would notice the dark circles under her eyes and surmise that she was tired. The truly intuitive might even be able to read a mild distress in her features. Even the best of them could not see the truth, though. She was sure that no one saw her real struggle. She felt like she was treading dark water. Pretty soon her head would go under and her throat would fill with fluid. She would kick and flail until her face could breach the surface, and she would spit out liquid grief and then gasp for life only to be pulled under again. Yes, she was drowning, and no one seemed to notice.

Daniel's fork clinked against his plate. He grabbed Zoe's hand and asked, "What's wrong?"

"The Devil wants me to help him open the gates of Hell—and I have a math test tomorrow," she quipped.

"Your sarcasm is duly noted. But you know what I mean," he continued, refusing to let it go. "I know you aren't okay, or fine, or just tired, or whatever other word you think you can use to make this conversation go away."

"We've been over this, Daniel. I'm the Daughter and—"

"And it's hard, and no one understands, and you're scared. Yeah, we have been over this, and I am going to tell you the same thing I told you last time—you need to find your faith. You have to let hope back in, Zo. You aren't alone in this fight, but none of us can do that for you."

Daniel's words stung her ears. His tone was cooler than she would have liked. Where was the sympathy? Where was the gentle touch and the soothing feel?

As if he'd read her thoughts, he squeezed her hand and said, "It's time to fight back."

Zoe jerked her hand back. *How dare he?* "I have been fighting!"

"No, you've been pouting. You've been cowering in a corner acting like you've already lost," Daniel said. He dropped his gaze and paused for a second, softening his demeanor. "Lucas died and that was horrible," he continued, "but losing him doesn't mean we lost everything." Daniel pushed his chair back, picking up their plates as he stood. He scraped the remnants of dinner into the garbage and began to rinse the dishes.

That's it? That's all he's going to say? There had been none of the sweetness and gentleness Zoe had become used to from Daniel, and it was jarring. What was she supposed to do with this? She wanted to yell at him, to tell him he had no right to talk to her that way. But, what way was that? He hadn't yelled. He hadn't been cruel, not really. The perceived cruelty, she realized, was that he was right. The moment Lucas's body had dropped into the snow, she had given up. She didn't know how to start over, or if that was even a possibility.

Zoe closed the white flaps of the Chinese food cartons and carried them to the refrigerator. She took her time placing them into the empty spaces between condiment bottles and half empty juice containers. She wanted to say something to Daniel but everything that came to mind felt wrong. Should she apologize? Should he? Should she ask for help? Why was it so hard to ask for help? They were supposed to have a nice dinner together. They were supposed to make each other laugh and forget about Hell and the reaping and death. She wanted to forget those things, to have a normal evening again.

Zoe closed the refrigerator at the same time that Daniel clicked the dishwasher shut. She stared at him, still unable, or unwilling, to speak.

Daniel dried his hands then walked the two steps to her. He brushed her hair back. "I believe in you," he told her as he leaned in, his lips pressing softly against hers.

Zoe wrapped her arms around him, nestling in as close as was possible. Her cheek brushed the soft flannel of his shirt. She drank in his musky, sweet scent. "I don't know what to do. I'm too weak...maybe it isn't me, or at least it shouldn't be."

His breath warmed the top of her head. "You're right, maybe it shouldn't be you." He pulled back to kiss her again. "And, you do know what to do." With a soft smile and one final kiss to her forehead, he said goodnight, grabbing his jacket off the back of a chair on his way out the back door.

Zoe stared at the space he left empty. She could hear Claire and Michael's muffled voices in the living room. What were they talking about? Was it her or Abaddon...Alex maybe? Claire's melodic laughter lilted down the short hallway drawing out Zoe's curiosity. She tiptoed along the wall and peeked in on the couple.

The two were sitting close together on the couch. A movie was playing on the flat screen, and Claire was trying to explain it to the Guardian. "She doesn't realize it's Wesley," she was saying.

"But how can she not tell? The mask only conceals half of his face. Did she not love this man? Should she not recognize his voice? If he loves her, why does he not just tell her the truth?" Michael asked, looking very serious and confused.

"All valid questions," Claire agreed and giggled again. "Your reaction is why. It makes for a little tension and suspense. Also, remind me never to watch Superman with you. You won't get past the glasses."

Zoe stifled her own chuckle. This was nice. If she couldn't have a normal night herself, she was glad at least Claire could. Though it was a little weird seeing her this way with Michael. Okay, a lot weird. Weird, but good.

Zoe turned on her heel, retreating to the stairs before they noticed her and invited her to join them. She didn't want to intrude on the moment, bringing her despair with her. She didn't want to carry it anymore period. It had been long enough, she decided. It was time to stop feeling sorry for herself.

Zoe closed her bedroom door. She knelt beside her bed and clasped her hands together, thinking maybe this would help—the ritual of it, the gestures of piety. Perhaps the position of her body could somehow direct the position of her mind and heart. She opened her mouth expecting words to spill out like a fountain. They were there inside her; she could feel them swirling and spinning. Thoughts, feelings, questions, supplications...she just needed to reach out and grip one tight enough to push it out of her mouth, but they kept slipping away. The words were all stuck, but apparently the tears were not. They slid down her cheeks and dripped on her saintly-poised hands. The wood floor felt cold and hard against her knees.

Please help. The silent plea was all she could grab hold of. It circled through her over and over again until it was like she was choking on it. She pulled her fingers apart and pulled herself onto her bed. She buried her wet face into her pillow and cried herself to sleep.

* * *

The familiar mix of blood and smoke burned inside Zoe's nostrils. She hated that smell. She hated this dreamscape even more. She squeezed her eyes shut tighter, refusing to relent to the nightmare. She was kneeling on the ground that felt thick with soot. She let her head hang down; she would not look at the bodies she knew surrounded her. A few angry tears traced the line of her jaw and dripped off her chin. The fact that she was crying—again—only served to make her angrier. She was too tired for this. She had no patience for more of Abaddon's mind games. "Let's just get to it," she whispered.

This was the Destroyer's cue. This was the moment he was supposed to hiss his way into the conversation. Zoe expected to hear the crunch of his heavy steps in the dead grass and feel the air grow cold around her. Neither happened. There was no snaky echo, no chill across her skin—and it was unnerving. Where was Abaddon? Why was she here, if not for him to slither into her mind and crush what hope she might have left? Had she fallen so far that she had now become her own torturer?

Open your eyes.

Zoe vaguely recognized the voice that wasn't really a voice at all. It floated over the field and bounced around inside the chambers of her heart. It was loud but not audible.

"Who are you?" she asked. She thought she knew, but she still wanted assurance. Her heart told her that wasn't how it worked. She needed to obey, but she didn't want to. She didn't want to open her eyes only to see the death all around her. But she needed to have faith, so she forced herself to gaze upward.

In the distance, an intense light shattered the dingy clouds. She squinted, straining to watch as it filled the sky and then shrank into a form. Zoe blinked her eyes, adjusting them to the brightness. As the light moved closer, she realized it was not just some glowing orb, but rather had the silhouette of a man. He was tall and had a stalwart build, but she couldn't make out any other features. For a moment she was so taken with the form that the landscape had become a blur around her. As he moved closer, everything began to come back into focus, the charred ground popped with brilliant hues underneath his feet. The color spread like paint from an artist's brush covering a dirty old canvas with a new creation.

The figure reached the spot where Zoe was still kneeling just in front of the burned remains of the ancient tree. "Hello Zoe." His voice was deep and penetrating, calling to all the places inside her that felt broken.

"Maker?" Had He heard her? Had He finally come?

"I have always been right here, you just didn't see me," He replied.

The sound of His voice was still shaking things into place inside her, and it made her voice quiver when she said, "I wanted to."

"I know."

"I don't know what to do," she said, unsure if her words were meant to hold a question or a revelation.

"You just need to keep your eyes open. You have seen so much death, been so focused on it, that you have stopped seeing the potential for life." The Maker reached out His arm and extended His fingers toward the dead tree behind her.

Zoe watched the blackened bark of the hollow trunk dissolve into a rich brown. It spread until it covered the full remnant of the once glorious tree, then stretched beyond seen borders as new branches sprang outward. As the branches grew, new leaves began poking out along the twisted limbs. While the tree stretched tall and wide, the color also ran downward as green moss began spreading along the bark and then spilled into a blanket of emerald that went sprawling in all directions. The ash under Zoe's knees transformed into lush grass that continued to unfurl beyond her. The corpses had faded, and wildflowers now bloomed in their places. The gray sky had turned to a luminous blue. The taste of death had gone, and new life filled all of Zoe's senses.

The Maker lowered His hand. "Death is not stronger than life. It is not stronger than love," He said.

"Love is supposed to defeat Abaddon?" Zoe asked.

"Not yours…" The Maker knelt in front of her. He lifted her chin with His finger. "…but mine."

"What does that mean? I want to understand, but I…" Zoe's doubts and fears fought back against the Maker's voice.

"You are trying to fight by yourself. You think the power is yours; it isn't. It never was. It is inside you, but it is not for you to wield, rather it is for you to receive and relinquish. Let go of control. Don't try to do. Just be."

"Be what?"

"Loved," The Maker answered. He wiped a tear from Zoe's cheek. "Darling Daughter, to love is hard—to walk around as one who is loved can be harder still. You must see that you are enough. You have always been enough. I cannot make you believe that. It is the one thing you must do on your own, but I do believe in you."

The Maker reached out His hand again. Zoe stared at it. Heat radiated from Him and washed over her, wrapping itself around her like a blanket. It seeped through her clothes and into her skin, moving deeper and deeper inside. She felt the cracks in her soul being seamed back together. The deep wells that she thought had gone dry sprang to life. If He could have faith in her, then how could she not have faith in return? Is this what it meant to be chosen? It wasn't a weight to carry; it was an identity. It was to be valued. To be loved. She felt this truth in her bones. She had been looking at everything all wrong. She had let her enemy feed her lies, and she had swallowed them. No more!

Zoe took the Maker's still-waiting hand. As soon as her skin made contact with His, the familiar tingle began to flow through her. She could see white light dance under the surface, illuminating her veins and spreading over her entire body. It felt stronger than it had ever been—warm, bright. It beamed.

"I'm ready now," she said.

* * *

The alarm on Zoe's phone played a melody that got louder with each passing second. The music poked into her brain, pulling her from sleep. She could still feel the prickle dancing along the surface of her skin and warmth hovered behind her closed eyelids, and even though she couldn't see it herself, she knew that her eyes were white, a sign of the power inside her being renewed. When Zoe finally opened her eyes, the whole world looked different.

CHAPTER THIRTY

Abaddon stood outside the abandoned warehouse, staring up into the night sky. The stars had been shrouded by the black mass of demons that had been called from all corners of the Earth. They were now spiraling over their master's head in wait. Hundreds of them had been able to trickle through already, and thousands more were poised at the gates. He could feel them straining against the veil, ready to rip their way into this world. The concentration of their power was like a drug being pumped into Abaddon's veins and flooding his faculties. Every sense felt sharper, every muscle stronger. He inhaled the darkness and it was invigorating.

"You look pleased," Meredith's voice intruded on the moment.

Abaddon ran his hand through his hair and adjusted the collar of his shirt. "I am," said the Destroyer as he strode past her and back inside.

The click of her heels let him know she was following him. "Does that mean we are ready?" she called out after him.

"It means *I* am ready," Abaddon snapped. He stopped abruptly, spun on his heel and glared into Meredith's dark eyes. "And you and the boy had better be too." He saw her flinch ever so slightly at his words, and the stench of her fear filled his nostrils. He drew it in deep as he ran his finger through a strand of her ebony hair.

"We are," Meredith responded, her voice wavering.

"Good."

"What's good?" Alex asked as he entered the room from a back doorway.

Abaddon stifled the growl that was forming at the back of his throat. This boy had taken more patience and mercy than he would normally offer a sad mortal, but he could still be of some use. That notion was the only reason he kept Alex alive. Abaddon knew he would still be a weakness to the Armor-Bearer, that his presence would distract her at least. He was counting on it.

"The time. That is what's good. I am ready to put our plans into action," Abaddon said, glancing at Alex over his shoulder. "We will end this tomorrow."

Alex's eyes widened as he asked, "Tomorrow?"

"Do you have other plans?" Abaddon punctuated his question with a snarl.

"No," Alex answered quickly and took a half step backward. "I just thought there would be more notice…"

"He just wants to make sure he's ready," Meredith sniveled softly, "so that things go the way you want."

"Things will go exactly like I have planned. The Daughter is weak. She will relent and the gates will open, and this will all be over, and you two can go back to your sad little lives." Abaddon spit the words out. His frustration was mounting, but now was not the time to lose his temper, to reveal his hand. He straightened his tie and the rolled cuffs of his shirt. "Do like you have been told, and when this is all over, everyone gets what they want."

"And Claire?" Alex asked.

"I won't lay a hand on her," Abaddon replied, catching the reflection of his smirk in his mirror. "But…" he regarded Alex, "will it matter if the Guardian remains at her side? You could end up so close and yet so far away from the object of your desire." He returned to the mirror, his smirk widening into a satisfied grin. "That would be a shame."

"I am sure it will all work out like it is meant to," Meredith cooed at Alex. She slinked around him, running her hand up his arm and over his chest. Abaddon was impressed with her ease at manipulation, at least as much as he could be impressed with a human. Really, he loathed them all.

The Destroyer retired to his reading chair. "You should both get some rest for the big day," he said as a means of dismissal. He wanted to be alone, away from them.

"Is there nothing else you need from us?" Meredith inquired. "Should we bait the trap?"

Abaddon flipped open one of his books. "No bait will be necessary, only an invitation."

"Would you like us to deliver it?" she offered.

Her questions and desperation were growing tiresome. The Destroyer tensed, ready to yell, to drive them out of his presence so that he could relish in his coming victory in silence, but he paused long enough to calm his words and quiet his tone. "No, I will handle that myself."

The two bowed in compliance and exited quickly.

Abaddon reclined in his chair. The darkness leaked in through the roof and walls. He could feel it like a tide that ebbed and flowed with the storm of demons above him. The power in him grew with each wave. Yes, tomorrow would be the culmination of all that he had spent several millennia devising. The taste of his coming victory was thrilling.

CHAPTER THIRTY-ONE

Zoe snuck downstairs, tiptoeing along the wood floor to avoid creaking planks so she wouldn't wake Claire. She grabbed the Chronicle from its box by the sofa and then crept back to her room and plopped on her bed, legs crossed with the book in front of her. She leaned over and retrieved the key, which she hadn't touched in weeks, from the bedside table drawer. With a click of the lock, the book seemed to breathe as a gasp of air set it into motion, and the leaves retracted into oblivion, allowing Zoe to open it and thumb through the worn pages.

From the moment she woke up, she had been drawn to the Chronicle. She wondered what it was she was supposed to be looking for. Was there some passage they had missed that would clarify everything? Was she even in need of clarification? Her mind felt focused for the first time since Lucas had died. The heaviness she had been carrying was gone. It was a bit surreal. Could it really be this simple, like a switch being flipped and that was it? Some voice inside told her there had to be more to it than this. Months' worth of grief and pain and fear couldn't just fade overnight. Could it? Was that the power of the Maker?

A knot began to twist in Zoe's stomach. All this time she had allowed her enemy to rule her thoughts and emotions. She had given in to him and let his nasty notions consume her when all she had to do was surrender her pain and herself to the Maker. It made her sick to think of the time and energy she had wasted that could have served a better purpose.

Warm air gusted through the room around Zoe and over the book, tossing its pages. Fading ink swirled on the parchment, Hebrew morphing into English. Zoe scanned the words that appeared. She had read them before. She had read the entire book before, but it was like she was only now really seeing the truth, not of a prophecy or calling, but of their humanity.

The battle had been arduous. With every shadow squelched, three more would rise, with molten giants also emerging beside them. The darkness felt consuming, unending. When the sun finally rose, there was only ash and blood remaining—ash and blood and heaviness. Ishbaal and Eleazer each took to a different direction to survey neighboring villages. Shammah ran to a nearby cave.

Shammah's skin was scarred from countless encounters with the demons he feared he would never escape. His mind was equally marred. He fell to his knees and cried out to the Maker. He asked for a release from this calling.

There it was right in front of her. One of the Three—giving up, or at least wanting to. And he was a warrior, unmatched in courage and skill. She kept reading.

Days passed in that cave. Shammah didn't eat or drink. He thought death would find him. But in the darkness of his isolation, it was not death that found him, but life. He yielded to hope, and it renewed him.

"Well, that sounds awfully familiar," Zoe mumbled to herself, then flipped a few more pages.

Eleazer cradled his firstborn in his arms, the life draining from the boy's body as blood trickled from his nose and mouth. His son's first battle against the shadows would be his last. Eleazer roared, and the primal cry shook the earth around them. He dropped his sword on the ground, picked up his dead child, and began to carry him home.

His brothers, Shammah and Ishbaal, retrieved the blade and followed Eleazer. They were silent the rest of the journey. After the burial, they stood by Eleazer as he screamed at Heaven. When he collapsed to his knees, they gave him back his abandoned sword. Eleazer took it, and they helped him to his feet.

Zoe read more and more of these hidden passages filled with pain and grief and doubt and fear. They were familiar, but she hadn't felt them before. Now she could relate to their suffering; it was the same as hers. She saw their humanity, and in it, saw herself. How was it disguised before? Her own perceptions of heroism and strength had masked the reality. Pain finds everyone, even the strong, even the called. She needn't be ashamed it had found her, and she wouldn't feel guilty for what she could not undo. Guilt served no purpose. Everything else could be redeemed because everything else could teach her something about herself, about her mission. She was stronger now for having suffered. Like the Three before her, she had yielded to hope, and it had renewed her.

Even now, it coursed through her veins. The heat of a power that was not her own pulsed through her body to the rhythm of her heartbeat. It was no longer hidden, needing to be coaxed to the surface. The light wasn't waiting on her to strain and push and beg. It was simply there, electrifying and calming all at once. It was life flowing through every part of her, and it left no room for doubt.

The clanging of pans and bowls in the kitchen caught Zoe's attention. She closed the Chronicle and headed downstairs, wrapping her fleece blanket around her as she went.

"That's not enough blueberries," Claire's voice bounced up the stairs.

"You never think there are enough blueberries," Michael responded.

"Is there really such a thing as *enough* when it comes to blueberries in muffins?" Claire popped a berry in her mouth. "Hey Zo, good morning," she said as Zoe made her way into the kitchen.

Claire's face was beaming brightly as she leaned on the counter next to Michael who was stirring batter in a large purple bowl.

"Wait a minute, he...the Guardian...the angel...he cooks?" Zoe asked, peering into the bowl before taking a seat at the counter.

"No. He...the Guardian...the angel...bakes," Claire said, giggling.

"How am I just finding out about this?" Zoe asked as she stole her own blueberry.

Michael took the blueberry carton from them and added more to the batter. "I do not understand why my baking skills are of such interest to the two of you," he said.

"Baking skills?" chirped Maggie who had just come skipping into the kitchen. "I'd say I'm sorry to barge in without knocking, but you gave me a key, so I'm not sorry. Also—good morning. Now whose baking skills are we interested in?"

"His," Zoe said nodding her head in the direction of the Guardian.

"Whoa, you bake?" Maggie asked Michael. "This is weird. Are these muffins gonna be magic? Is there some angelic hoodoo in them?" She dipped her finger in the batter, sniffed it, and then licked it clean.

"I do not know what hoodoo is," Michael responded. "These

muffins are blueberry, just blueberry." He pulled the bowl away from the girls and began to pour the batter into the paper-lined pan.

"Well, can you at least zap them or something so they bake in like thirty seconds?" Maggie asked, batting her eyelashes. "I'm hungry."

"I cannot."

Zoe laughed as Maggie pouted at the angel's curt response. Her disappointment only seemed to last for a moment before her eyes flitted to Claire, and a curl played at the corner of her mouth. "What about—"

"No," Claire interrupted. "There will be no pity eggs today. You want eggs, you fix them yourself."

"Boo," Maggie said, returning to her pouting.

Zoe giggled. "I know what will cheer you up," she whispered to Maggie. "Claire, watch any good movies lately?"

Claire's eyes widened and her cheeks flushed a rose tone. She was caught and apparently had no way to escape. She sighed. "Actually, Michael and I watched one of my favorites last night. I thought it was time he was introduced to *The Princess Bride*."

Maggie slapped her hands flat on the counter, gaping at Zoe and Claire and Michael. Her entire face was lit with mirth. "Really? I am sorry I missed that....so, so, so sorry." Maggie wasn't even trying to hide her amusement. Upon meeting Claire's glare, she regained her composure enough to clear her throat and add, "It's one of my favorites too. I would have loved to have watched it with you."

"Watch what?" Daniel asked as he entered the room. He placed his customary kiss on Zoe's cheek.

"*The Princess Bride*. Claire and Michael watched it last night," Zoe said trying hard to bite back the giggle fighting its way out at the sight of her aunt's embarrassment.

Daniel's smirk grew as he teased, "Claire and Michael huh?"

Claire was staring at Zoe. *I will get you for this*, she mouthed.

"And now Michael is baking blueberry muffins for breakfast," Maggie interjected.

Daniel's mouth gaped open. "Wait a minute—you bake?" he asked the Guardian. "Where has this talent been for the last three years? I'm a growing boy. I like muffins too."

Michael had put the muffins in the oven and was leaning against the sink. He appeared to survey Claire for a moment, and then he crossed his arms over his chest and squinted at Daniel. Zoe could have sworn his eyes sparkled, and she thought a smirk of his own was lying just beneath the surface of his stoic features. "I like her better than you," the angel replied.

Claire clamped her hand over her mouth to quiet the laugh that erupted. Maggie just laughed, not caring to conceal it. Daniel's jaw dropped, and he stepped back, slightly deflated.

Zoe bit her bottom lip to hide her grin. She took Daniel's hand in hers and leaned her head on his shoulder and said, "I like you enough to make you muffins. Does that help?"

"A little... I guess," Daniel huffed. "But can I just say, I don't like it when he gets all—all human—and sarcastic. I like him better when he's weird and robotic."

"No, you don't. You just don't like being the target of his snark," Zoe said and kissed his cheek.

"Can we get back to this movie thing?" asked Maggie. "I want to watch a movie with Michael. I need to see this in action." She opened the fridge and grabbed the juice. "What should he see next? I vote *The Goonies*... Or *Breakfast at Tiffany's*... Ooh, Ooh, *Independence Day!*"

"Those are the most random movie choices ever," Daniel said as he got glasses out of the cabinet.

Michael leaned closer to Claire. "What is a Goonie?" he asked. The room fell silent for just a second before erupting into laughter again.

Claire composed herself and stared sweetly at Michael. "Just check those muffins, big guy. We'll worry about Goonies and alien attacks later."

Zoe thought she couldn't possibly laugh any harder until Michael, still looking confused, said, "I do not understand. Should we not worry about any kind of attack now?"

Claire wrapped her arm around his and, lifting herself on her tiptoes, rested her chin on Michael's shoulder. "Awe, sweetie," she said, smiling up at him. "This particular attack can wait until our next movie night. I promise. Now, seriously, check the muffins."

Zoe was glad to see the sweetness between Claire and Michael. She was glad to have her family find enjoyment together again. This was what she envisioned a morning as a normal family to be like. It had been too long since they had one. Others had come close, but fear had always loomed. Heaviness had always encumbered everything, even amidst small joys. But not today. There was no dark cloud, only the silver lining. Zoe reveled in it. She wasn't drowning beneath the weight of fear, but floating, held up by love. Love for her family and for Daniel. Love from her Maker. She knew it wouldn't take away what was to come, and that it wouldn't stop the darkness from attacking again. It wasn't a mirage masking reality, but a new perspective on it. Zoe was happy for it. And she was happy to see her aunt walk in a new freedom herself. She was just happy and would not let needless worry steal it away anymore.

CHAPTER THIRTY-TWO

The clang of swords and the hum of conversation reverberated through the planks of the barn door. Claire slid the heavy thing open to reveal a merry scene. Merry because it was full of people. That idea still felt so strange to her. She had never thought there would be a time when she would be surrounded by friends and family, all fighting together. Family had always been something she'd kept separate from the field of battle, and it was her biggest regret. While it hadn't been wholly her fault she had been isolated, she couldn't help but wish things had been different. But regrets were of no use. The path she'd traveled had helped build her, and she was far from perfect, but she liked who she had become.

"About time you all showed up. We've been at this since right after sunup," Charlie said as he fired a shot at one of the targets.

Levi loaded his own crossbow. "Leave them alone," he said. "We only got started that early because the coffee ran out."

"Well, we come bearing more coffee and muffins," Claire said, dropping her duffel and gesturing toward Zoe and Maggie who were behind her with thermoses and a basket.

All activities stopped as the descendants dropped their

weapons and gathered around the girls, clamoring for the fresh-baked goodness.

Charlie brought a muffin to his mouth, but hesitated. "Who baked these?"

"I did," Michael replied from behind Claire.

Claire watched as the huddle at the thermoses all turned in unison to stare at the angel.

"I baked and I do not wish to talk about it further," Michael said.

There were a few nods of concession, and the group proceeded to chow down.

"Feeling better today?" Claire asked Levi who was pouring himself a cup of steaming coffee.

"Much," Levi responded, then sipped the drink cautiously. "Thanks again," he said, raising his mug toward Michael.

"It was not all my doing," Michael replied.

"Your *doing* was a lot though. But, yeah, Sue and her herbal concoction is doing the trick with the rest. I'll be good as new in no time." Levi took another longer sip of coffee.

Zoe walked up with the basket and offered Levi a muffin. "I'm glad you're okay," she said. "I'm sorry you got hurt. I'm sorry for getting all of you involved in all this."

It warmed Claire's heart to see Levi reach his wrinkled hand over and touch Zoe's. "We were all involved in this long before you were born, sweetheart. You have nothing to apologize for." He smiled at her and took the baked good.

"But you all didn't have to come here or be this close to it," Zoe said, setting the basket down.

"Maybe not. But we're here now, and we don't regret it, and we aren't going anywhere," Levi responded. "In fact, we've called some friends. I bet more will be here before the week's out."

Claire put her hand on her niece's shoulder. "Thank you," she said, offering her words of gratitude to Levi and the others who were all standing circled around them.

Charlie stepped up, adjusting his hat as usual. "We don't need thanks. But a plan might be nice. If this is going to be the end, I say we be the ones who figure out how to end it."

"Agreed," Jack said and nodded.

Claire knew they were right. They had been letting Abaddon call all the shots, dictate all the moves, and it was time to stop playing defense and develop some offense. They needed to take the higher ground in this war. She tried to decipher the emotion on each of the faces that encircled her. Some eyes were tired. Some jaws were clenched. Fear showed around the edges of them all, but it was tempered by a steely determination. Passion blazed beyond the surface of each gaze. They knew what was at stake; they had counted the cost and were willing to pay it. One by one, Claire saw the grit in these warrior faces, including Zoe's. She looked deeper into her niece's eyes. The dark circles had vanished. The glaze of grief had all but disappeared, and Zoe's hazel eyes were bright again.

Claire addressed the group. "You all are right, it's time we take charge. But are we ready?" The question was directed more to Zoe than anyone else.

"I am." Zoe's reply was quiet, calm.

Claire took her niece's hand. "You sure?" she asked.

"I am," Zoe replied.

"What's changed?" Claire asked, taking note of Zoe's breaking smile, one she hadn't seen in quite a while.

Zoe let go of Claire's hand and reached into the large duffel bag that had been momentarily forgotten on the floor. She unsheathed the Eden Sword. "I was reminded of who I am and who I'm not. I know where the power comes from," she said, "and knowing that lifted away the weight I had been letting suffocate me."

The last words were barely out of Zoe's mouth when she closed her eyes and reopened them to reveal their solid white glow. It traveled through her veins, unmistakable under her skin, until it reached the golden sword in her hand. The light flowed into it, illuminating the metal. Everyone stared. There was no flickering. There was no hesitation. The power inside her seemed to gush out like a dam had been broken. Seeing this released something in Claire. The bits of fear and regret she had been holding on to dissolved under the glow of Zoe's light. She had not failed. She truly and wholly believed that now.

Claire watched her niece smile wide. Zoe blinked again, and the light was gone. "How's that for control?" Zoe asked Michael.

The Guardian bowed his head with a pleased expression.

"Well, then, let's put together a plan," Charlie said clapping his hands, and the descendants began to disperse back throughout the barn.

Claire wrapped her arms around Zoe, hugging her tight. "I'm proud of you, Zo."

"I didn't do much...just let go," Zoe responded.

Claire gave her niece one more squeeze, whispering, "Letting go can be really hard."

* * *

Alex tossed and turned. The morning was shifting into afternoon, but he hadn't slept all night. In fact, since moving into the warehouse, he had barely slept in days. Fatigue went deeper than a mere lack of sleep though. Exhaustion sank through his muscles, inside his bones, and down deep into his spirit. Was this what power was supposed to feel like?

You'll get used to it. This is just temporary. It'll be over soon. You just need to give in, to let go.

Remnants of Meredith's voice, her prior reassurances, replayed inside his brain, but they did little to offer any real comfort. He was restless. His soul was unsettled, a nomad wandering inside him.

Alex threw off his blanket and lowered his bare feet onto the cold concrete floor. It used to bother him, the cold; he would retract at the feel of it. Now it was his normal, an adaptation that he hated. He craved warmth.

Alex turned on the faucet and waited for the water to heat

enough to offer some pleasure against his skin. He cupped his hands under the stream and then splashed his face. He rubbed his eyes until his blurry vision cleared and he was staring at his pale reflection in the cloudy mirror. His eyes were dim, bordered by dark circles and deepening lines. He thought he looked sick. But he knew he was really just sad. Was this worth it? Would it ever be worth it? A splintered heart had driven him to a much more broken place.

It's about choosing what's right.

Claire. Her words, her voice, her face. Thoughts of her gave him fewer and shorter moments of solace.

She doesn't love you. She never loved you. Meredith's whispers returned.

She did...or she didn't. What was the point of wondering? There was no going back, no return or recovery from what he had done, who he was becoming, what he would have to do. He hated her and loved her. And he hated himself for both. Perhaps Meredith was right about that; he just needed to let go. But letting go was so hard.

CHAPTER THIRTY-THREE

A dozen pizza boxes were scattered across the battered old farm table they had brought into the barn. Zoe liked the look of it; a makeshift family space surrounded by their makeshift family, littered with the piles of journals Claire had sent her and Daniel to get from the house. Since her display that morning, Zoe and the others had been busy building a battle strategy. Cornering the devil wouldn't be easy.

"We're going to need help," Charlie said, taking a long drink of water from his tin cup. He set it down and leaned back in his chair, scratching his stubble.

"Help is coming...hopefully soon," Claire said, turning to Michael for something, maybe reassurance. The Guardian dipped his head in a wary nod.

Bobby tossed a half-eaten pizza crust back into a grease-stained box. "I got a call from the Wilsons. They're bringing a caravan," he said. "Should be here in two days."

"Reverend Larson is heading in too," Thomas added. "But what do we do when they get here?"

"How are we going to get the upper hand? We still need Abaddon to gather his minions to break down the veil enough for the gates to open," Catherine interjected. "That's the only way Zoe can force them all back in and seal the doors."

Levi stretched and rubbed the back of his neck. "She's right. Abaddon isn't naive. He won't fall into a trap," he said.

Zoe had listened quietly to all the talk. They knew how to kill demons of every variety. They would be ready for praetors and hounds. They could hold their own against the proselytes. The devil himself was the trick. He wasn't naïve; that was true. "But he's arrogant," Zoe whispered into the conversation.

Silence circled the table and all eyes turned to the Daughter.

Zoe fidgeted slightly in her seat. "Abaddon isn't naive—you're right, but he is arrogant," she repeated. "He thinks he's already won—"

"Haven't I though?" The husky melody of Abaddon's voice crawled into the room with a cloud of smoke which shifted into human form right before their eyes.

Before skin could fully encapsulate the dark cloud, all of the descendants had already pulled their weapons and were poised for attack.

The Destroyer sneered and said, "It's adorable that you think any of you could stop me. Heaven's strongest failed at that task long ago."

Michael stepped forward with his blade in hand. "They did not fail. They cast you out."

"And why?" Abaddon asked. "Why was I removed from my position? Pride? Desire? I am not so different from all of you. I wanted to matter, but you—you meager beings—became the dream, the favored creation."

The Guardian twisted his sword in his hand. Zoe watched his eyes grow brighter, and the light begin to pulse in his chest as he said, "You wanted power that did not belong to you."

"It should have been mine," Abaddon snapped. His eyes lit up like fire and then faded to black. "Why does this world, these things, get to come first? I am merely righting a wrong." His voice calmed as he turned directly to Zoe and said, "You can help me. Really you *will* help me."

The heat was beginning to rise inside Zoe, and she pushed it down, not wanting to reveal her new truth to her enemy just yet. She clenched her jaw and said, "I won't."

"We will see about that." Abaddon's wicked laugh echoed off the rafters as he returned to black smoke that retreated from the room just as they heard sirens blare in the distance.

"What are those?" Zoe asked.

"Tornado sirens," Maggie replied.

"I don't think a tornado is really what's coming," Daniel said, running to the doorway. Zoe and Maggie followed.

The sunset sky was further darkened by a swarm of shadows gathering over the town.

"It looks like this is happening whether we are ready or not," Maggie said, taking Zoe's hand.

"I'm ready," Zoe replied and squeezed her friend's fingers in her own. "But Maggie, you don't have to—"

"I'm coming. Don't try and stop me. It won't be pretty," she warned. "There will be screaming, and hysterics the likes of a toddler tantrum, and it'll be embarrassing for both of us."

"We wouldn't want that," Zoe said and smiled. This wasn't a patrol though, and her insides were screaming at her to make Maggie stay behind. But that wasn't her choice. Maggie was every bit as chosen as Zoe had been. In some ways she had been better at it, more ready than Zoe herself. "Just be careful, and watch your back," she relented.

"I'll be rock formation ready if things go sideways, cross my heart." And Maggie did just that, her index finger drawing an X across her chest like she always did.

"Get your weapons ready," Claire shouted. She came up behind Zoe and grabbed her arm. "You good?" she asked.

"Yep," Zoe assured her, taking up the Eden Sword.

"Then let's go," Claire called out, jogging toward her SUV. Zoe and the others followed.

The sky was getting darker by the second. Thunder rattled around them and the ground shook. Zoe turned her golden sword, its tip pointing upward. A hint of light glinted off the blade's edge. It wasn't from the falling sun but from Zoe, her luminous eyes reflecting in the metal. Yes, she was ready, and for the first time, her enemy would not be. She was their upper hand.

The sirens still whirred as Zoe and the descendants arrived in town. She saw police and firefighters evacuating people from the streets, urging them to seek shelter from a threat they couldn't yet see. Claire's SUV skidded to a halt behind the library. The other descendants came up behind them in their own beaten up vehicles. They all hopped out, weapons in hands.

"Looks like they are right above us," Jack said as he stared up at the blackened sky.

This was all too familiar to Zoe. "We are close. Abaddon will be just in front of the courthouse," she said.

"How can you be so sure?" Claire asked.

"Call it a hunch." Zoe knew Claire was smarter than that, but bringing up her nightmares would do no good now. Abaddon would jump at that chance himself. This was all staged, an effort to drive her fears to the surface and weaken her mind. She wouldn't let it work.

"Let's split up then," Claire commanded, rotating her sword like she always did to warm up her muscles before sparring. "Go in twos up the side streets and hold back everything you can so Zoe can do her thing."

Each nodded or grunted their understanding and agreement as the pairs dispersed. Billy and Bobby charged up the alleyway by the Haven. Thomas and Catherine followed Sue and Jack down the back avenue to cover the other side of the main street.

Charlie and Levi snuck toward the fire escape of a building.

Levi pulled the ladder down and called to Maggie, "You're

with us sweetheart. We're gonna perch on the rooftop and pick off what we can."

"I like that plan," Maggie said as she jogged off to meet her partners.

Me too. Zoe was more than a little relieved by that news. Maggie wasn't completely out of danger, but she was now less likely to end up bleeding out on the curb. "Kill lots of the things," Zoe called after her friend.

Maggie turned, saluted, and proceeded up the ladder.

"I'm with you," Daniel said taking Zoe's hand.

She glanced down at their intertwined fingers, and the scene of him being dragged away by shadows played in her mind. Zoe closed her eyes and pushed the nightmarish images away. "I wouldn't have it any other way," she said pushing up on her toes to kiss him. "Let's go."

Daniel nodded and led her toward the main street. They hadn't even turned the corner fully before demons were clawing at them. She and Daniel sliced through them, working to get closer to the courthouse. A swirl of smoke and shadows had darkened the sky above them. Brimstone burned her nostrils. It wasn't exactly like her dream, but it was close.

Arrows whizzed overhead, picking off shadows, aiding the descendants on the ground. In her peripheral vision, Zoe could see the others hacking through the demons that were charging down the street. The force of such a huge throng had brought down the electrical lines, which now sparked in the road. One of the shop's windows had been broken and another shop had caught on fire. Zoe could hear the hellhounds howling. A pack of them was running down the sidewalk and along the walls of the buildings that lined it, all headed toward Michael. The Guardian's electric wings contrasted with the black that swarmed around him and Claire as they fought side by side, as one.

Zoe and Daniel pushed closer to the front line. The ground shook as praetors emerged, the large beasts looming just behind Abaddon and his proselytes.

The Destroyer smiled at Zoe as she and Daniel approached. "Meredith, be a dear and take Alex to deal with the Armor-Bearer and her Guardian if you will. I have a date with the Daughter. Come closer now, dear," he said to Zoe. Abaddon's true molten form emerged as he shed the skin of Mr. Achan. "I want to smell the sweet stench of your fear."

The hoard of shadows in front of Zoe and Daniel parted giving her a clear path to her enemy. She squeezed Daniel's hand and said to him, "Go help the others."

"Are you sure? I don't want to leave you alone to face him," Daniel said pulling her gaze to him.

"I'm not alone," Zoe whispered.

Daniel took off, slashing through the black mass to get to Jack and Sue who seemed to be struggling to keep on their feet.

Zoe continued forward, taking each step with care. She inhaled and exhaled slow, deep breaths, working to stay in control and to keep the heat inside her at bay.

"Do you recognize it? The end?" Abaddon asked her. What little light there was glinted off his black teeth.

"There's less screaming in this version," Zoe replied.

"The screaming will come soon." The Destroyer lifted his hand, and the lava in his veins burned brighter. The hounds wailed again.

Zoe could see that Claire and Michael were being pushed toward the grand steps of the old courthouse. A gang of shadows was moving to pin them in, Meredith and Alex pulling their strings. Michael swung at a hound, cutting it open. Another howled as an arrow pierced its shoulder, and then it fell to the ground and dissolved. Meredith growled and drew more shadows out from under the asphalt street. Claire was cutting them down as quickly as they rose.

Zoe kept walking toward Abaddon but couldn't take her eyes off the skirmish. Her stomach twisted watching it. Fear pushed upward, but Zoe wouldn't let it stop her.

Michael roared as a devil dog's claws scratched across his chest.

Alex pushed another round of demons toward the Guardian. Zoe cringed as they pounced on the angel, pushing him to the ground.

She heard Claire yell and watched her run up the three steps that separated her aunt and the angel. Claire beat the shadows off of Michael enough for him to get back on his feet. His chest was bloody but Zoe noted that his eyes glowed brighter.

"You don't have to do this, Alex," Claire shouted over the noise of the battle. "We don't have to be on opposite sides here."

"It's too late for changing minds," Alex yelled as he thrust his hand forward and four more demons charged toward Michael.

"It's never too late," Claire replied. She never stopped fighting through the creatures that had encircled her and Michael.

"Is it getting too familiar, Zoe?" Abaddon laughed, drawing Zoe's attention back to him.

"If you only knew all the ways this was different from that nightmare," Zoe said as she spun the Eden Sword in her hand. She was less than ten feet from Abaddon, from ending all of this.

Then she heard Maggie scream from the roof behind her.

Zoe jerked around and saw that Maggie was hastily loading another arrow while repeatedly glancing toward the courthouse.

Zoe spun around, looking back toward the stairs. Alex was pushing more shadows toward Michael, his eyes trained on the angel. Michael was falling under the weight of the attack. Claire had been cut off from her Guardian. She was frantically trying to push her way through, her sword slicing through the wall of demons that separated them. She couldn't see what was coming.

"Claire!" Zoe yelled.

Claire didn't see it, the smoke mixed in among the shadows. Her aunt was fighting valiantly against more demons than anyone else could possibly handle, but she didn't see the thing coming for her.

Zoe wrapped her fingers tighter around the grip of her sword.

She stepped to the left, ready to veer from her course to help Claire.

A rock hand grabbed her by the neck. "Now I can't let you stop the fun," Abaddon said and sneered, "but I don't want you to miss it either." He held her in place, forcing her to watch.

Just behind Claire, the smoke gathered and grew into a female silhouette. Meredith's dark hair blew around her pale skin as she drew her long sword.

"No!" Alex called to his partner.

Meredith grinned wickedly, then thrust her blade into Claire's back. The Armor-Bearer jerked forward with the impact, then back when Meredith removed the bloody sword.

Claire dropped to the ground, a slow motion fall on the steps. Her head hit the concrete and bounced once. Blood trickled from her mouth and out of her wound, painting everything around her red. Her sword fell from her hand and rolled down two steps.

A blue pulse emanated from Michael's hand. It was enough to dissolve the demons that hadn't yet dispersed on their own.

"No," Zoe gasped, frozen. Tears blurred her vision. It had all happened so fast. She hadn't had time to think or react.

"Let's end this," Abaddon said. "Just give up, and give me what I want. You're too weak to beat me."

Zoe felt the heat rise. It beat inside her chest, pulsing outward in flashes of light through her veins. "I wouldn't be so sure," Zoe said. She gazed into the Destroyer's inky eyes and caught the reflection of her own, blazing white, and her skin lit by the power that had lined every inch of her.

Abaddon grumbled, dropping her and pulling his hand back like it was in pain.

"You want to end this?" Zoe lifted the Eden Sword and the light in her began to travel into the blade. "Ok, let's end it."

The beast growled and stepped back.

Zoe lunged forward, but the Destroyer dissolved into smoke and retreated, his proselytes and demons following.

CHAPTER THIRTY-FOUR

He saw it coming. Peering through the cracks of light that would break between the demons ravaging him, Michael saw the proselyte looming, floating, and then rising behind Claire. He saw it and could not stop it. Time moved too fast. The creatures clawing into his skin were too many. His mouth couldn't get words of warning out in time. The surge of power he needed in order to disintegrate the darkness and pull the Armor-Bearer to safety took seconds too long.

He saw the determination on Claire's face widen into shock as Meredith's sword plunged into her back. Blood trickled out of her mouth and dribbled along the curve of her lips. Her eyes locked with his for a short moment, too short, before they drifted closed and she fell forward onto the steps.

Then time stopped. Demons still shrieked, some in pleasure and some in pain. Zoe's scream echoed. Michael could feel the power within him surging, building, becoming a tidal wave of electricity that pulsed outward and decimated every demonic shadow within five hundred feet of him. The proselytes retreated in smoke. It was all happening; the world was still moving, but his world had stopped. Claire's heart had ceased beating, and it felt like his had stopped with it.

Michael jumped down the steps and slid onto his knees next to Claire. He placed his hands on her cheeks, hoping for some sign of life. She didn't breath. She didn't flinch. She didn't move. Clear droplets plopped onto his hand and Claire's cheek. Were they tears? Were they his? In all his existence, Michael had never cried. He had never been so affected by human emotions. They trembled through him, making him feel weak and sick. Pain twisted inside him, squeezing his stomach and lungs and heart so tightly he couldn't breathe. The pain traveled up and lodged in his throat. He pulled Claire's bloody body into his arms and cradled her against his chest. The pain pushed up further until it exploded in a gasp, which became a moan, which turned into a loud wail. It reverberated back, shaking him again.

All the sounds around him were nothing more than a buzz in his ears. Somewhere on the edge of his senses, Michael discerned the others were gathering around him. They didn't speak. They didn't reach out, or if they did, they stopped themselves before actually touching him or the Armor-Bearer. Did they feel like he did? Were they crumbling? He didn't want to look at them.

Michael wiped the blood from Claire's lip with his thumb. He brushed her hair off her face and studied its lines and curves. It didn't look like her anymore, not really. Her skin had lost its color. The spark in her eyes that made her *her* was gone. Her very soul was disappearing. He couldn't let her be gone.

"Michael?" A hand rested on his shoulder. He looked up at Zoe, her face was wet and flushed. Her mouth quivered like she wanted to say more, or scream, but she did neither.

No, he wouldn't let Claire be gone. Zoe needed her; they all needed her. They needed her more than they needed him.

Michael squeezed Zoe's hand, then removed it from his shoulder and said, "Stand back."

He glanced around him to be sure they had obeyed. When he was confident they stood clear, he looked at Claire again. He leaned close to her and whispered, "I love you." Then he kissed her forehead, letting his lips rest against her cold skin for just a moment.

As he raised his head back up, his wings emerged from his back. The blue of their light reflected off Claire's skin. Michael touched his hand to her heart and closed his eyes. *Please, let me do this... for her... for them... for You.*

Once he'd offered his silent prayer, Michael opened his eyes again. The light within him, a bright sapphire, illuminated his veins and spread over his entire body until his skin glowed. It radiated in waves, born in his heart, and pushed outward until Claire's chest began to hold the same cobalt gleam. The tide grew stronger. The light in her chest spread outward like a spiderweb, beyond her ribs, reaching the tips of her fingers. It moved across every inch of her, even up her neck, painting lines over her face.

Michael heard a collective gasp behind him. The Guardian smiled at the incandescent eyes that had thrust open. The body in his arms was becoming warmer, and color was returning to Claire's skin. He leaned forward again and placed a final kiss on her reddening lips. "I am sorry. I have to break my promise," he whispered. "I have to leave you again."

All the light faded. Claire's eyes closed again but her chest was rising and falling with new life. Michael set her gently back on the steps. He stood and gazed upward. *Thank you.*

They had been tethered and he had given the rest of himself so Claire could live. Michael would do it a hundred times over. He was glad to sacrifice himself for her. There was no greater way to express what he had felt for her for so long. She would live, and that gave him peace in his dying. He felt it—death. Weakness was all that remained inside his shuddering muscles. Michael felt his knees buckle and then he collapsed on the steps next to Claire. Everything went dark.

* * *

Abaddon let out an angry, feral groan as he flipped the table over, sending it crashing against the cement floor and splintering into pieces. "How did this happen? I had that girl right where I wanted her. She was weak. She was ready to give in!"

Had he underestimated her? What had he missed? It didn't matter now. The Maker had gotten to her, of that Abaddon was sure. His only solace was in the fact the Armor-Bearer was dead. Perhaps killing her would give him enough of a reprieve to salvage his plans.

"You said Claire wouldn't be hurt! You promised me—" Alex's stench filled the Destroyer's nostrils.

"I said I wouldn't lay a hand on her and *I* didn't," Abaddon, back in his human façade, replied as he ran his fingers through his disheveled hair, smoothing it back into place.

"But—"

Abaddon didn't let him finish his protest. He reached out his hand, thrusting Alex back against a concrete column, his feet dangling inches above the ground.

"I am tired of you," Abaddon said as he turned his hand slowly, tightening his invisible grip until Alex's body began to writhe in pain. "Your jealousy and pain no longer amuse me. Claire is gone and you serve no more purpose. We are done, you and I." With a flick of the Destroyer's wrist, Alex's neck cracked, and his body fell to the ground.

Meredith gasped.

"Do you have questions? Protests?" Abaddon asked his proselyte.

"N-no...no," she answered.

"Good. We must move quickly. I don't want to give them time to regroup."

CHAPTER THIRTY-FIVE

Something felt wrong. It was warm. There was a softness under her instead of the cold concrete and pooling blood that were the last things she could remember feeling before her vision had faded. Claire jerked fully awake. She patted her hand against her back and then her stomach, checking for a wound. There wasn't one. Her clothes were ripped and bloody but her skin was closed, smooth, as though nothing had happened. But she knew it had happened. She knew a sword had sliced through her and had ripped her apart. There was a phantom pain haunting her insides.

"Claire?" Zoe's whisper pulled her attention to her niece who was sitting on the coffee table.

They were home, in the living room. Claire realized she was on the couch. Daniel and Charlie were standing by the fireplace. Maggie was in the corner chair like always. Had she been crying? She appeared as if she had been crying. So did Zoe, who just watched silently as Claire took in the scene and tried to put the pieces together.

"What happened? Where's Michael?" Claire asked. She hadn't fully spoken his name before some piece of memory poked at her brain. Was it a memory? She couldn't see it, she couldn't see anything, but she could hear it, feel it. His voice. *I love you...I'm sorry... I have to leave you.* And then she remembered feeling power move through her like lightning. And a kiss. She touched her lips with the tips of her fingers. "Michael?"

"He...He's gone," Zoe replied.

"How exactly?" Claire already knew the answer. It was becoming clear to her what had happened. She knew Michael well enough to know what he must have done, but she needed to hear it out loud. She needed confirmation to prove her fears were correct. She hoped they weren't. *Please let me be wrong.*

"He gave himself up for you," Charlie answered. "Gave you the rest of his power so you could live." Charlie's voice was softer than usual, like it was playing at the edge of sadness but still trying to hide it. His puffy red eyes gave him away though.

Claire's chest tightened as she asked, "Where is he now?" She swallowed down the heartache that was trying to erupt in cries she wasn't ready to release.

It was Daniel who quietly answered her. "They took his body back to the barn."

"I need to see him," Claire said, moving to stand.

Zoe placed her hand on Claire's arm. "Aunt Claire, are you sure?"

Claire nodded.

"Then I'll take you," Zoe said, moving to her side.

"No, I need to go alone," Claire said. She took one step then leaned toward her niece. "I'm fine. I'll be fine. I need to do this myself. Please."

"Okay," Zoe agreed.

Claire adjusted her bloody shirt, picked up her car keys from the table, and walked out the door.

* * *

She sat in her SUV for thirty minutes, working up the courage to step inside that barn. She had seen some of the others walk in and out and around their tents and RVs. New vehicles had pulled in, but no one came close enough to offer any introductions. She guessed the look on her face must have been enough to keep them away because they saw her but didn't approach. Perhaps they just didn't know how to approach her, or what to say, or what to do. There really wasn't anything they could say or do. Claire decided distance was probably best at the moment. She didn't want to talk to anyone anyway. She wanted to see Michael. Really she wanted to see him alive. But he wasn't. Wanting it wouldn't change that, but she still needed to see him.

Finally, Claire got out of her car and walked into the barn. Michael's body had been laid on the same table they'd all gathered around earlier that day. Sue was standing over him, washing blood off his hands—Claire's blood. When the older woman saw Claire approaching, she put her cloth down in the bowl of water she'd been using, nodded silently to her, and headed to the door. She paused as she passed by Claire. She squeezed her hand briefly without saying a word, then continued out.

Claire stepped closer to Michael. She wanted to touch him. She reached out to but stopped. He would feel cold. When she touched him, this would all be made real, and there would be no denying it. She decided to give herself another second to believe he was just asleep, or whatever people tell themselves to stave off actuality. She imagined Michael would probably have told her that was unhealthy. She chuckled at the thought of his correction. She reached out again, letting her fingers graze a long strand of his hair. His gray flannel shirt was bunched so she smoothed it down. A red stain was smeared across his chest. Claire closed her eyes and placed her hand on it. He had held her there.

Inhale. Exhale. Eyes open. Claire prodded herself to come back to reality. She pulled a chair closer to the table and sat down. She picked up Michael's hand, held the back of it against her cheek, and then kissed it gently before laying it back on his chest. She didn't let go. She kept hold of him and let go of the tears. They were quiet streams, not the body-wracking sobs Claire would have expected. She wanted to break. She felt the cracking in her heart. But there was something else there too, something that felt like a hand, wrapping around it, holding it together. When she lost Alex, she'd felt regret and loneliness and fear with the sadness, but not now, not with this. Michael had sacrificed himself for her, and that was a greater love than she'd ever thought she deserved. Maybe real love is like that. It isn't about what we deserve. She had figured out that what she'd felt for Alex hadn't been real, or at least it hadn't been love, not the true kind that is selfless. She was sure now that real love is what she had felt for Michael because she would have done the same thing for him. She was also learning that kind of love wasn't something we came by ourselves. She wasn't capable of it on her own.

Warmth was welding her heart back together. It emanated out and wrapped around her. She was sure scars would remain; the seams would always show. She knew she would always think of Michael and miss him. There would be times when she would wish he was beside her. She would grieve him in her dreams. And also when something like muffins or the bracelet on her wrist reminded her of him. There would come a time, when this war was over and distractions were gone, when she would weep for him. This time the grief wouldn't kill her though. She understood that he had made sure she could stay so she could help Zoe, so she could live. And that was what she was going to do.

Claire moved Michael's fingers so they were between hers and then laid her head against his shoulder. His normal musk was tainted by the scent of her stale blood but she didn't care. Tomorrow, she would go back to all the things she had to do without him. Tomorrow, she would pick up a sword, and he wouldn't be there to fight beside her. But tonight, she would stay here next to him, one last time.

CHAPTER THIRTY-SIX

Zoe sent Charlie home close to midnight. He texted to let her know that her aunt was still at the barn. Daniel and Maggie had decided to stay the night so she wouldn't be alone. Somewhere around four in the morning, Claire had come home. Zoe heard her whisper to Daniel to go back to sleep before she came upstairs. Zoe got out of bed and peeked into the hall in time to see Claire close her bedroom door. A few minutes later she heard the shower start. She went back to bed and lay there, silent and awake, for close to an hour. She listened to Claire's every move. The water turning off. The creak of her bed when she'd climbed in. Zoe waited and listened, but there was nothing more. There were no sobs, no tossing and turning, no pacing the floor. She wasn't satisfied Claire was okay, but she would let it be for now and go back to sleep.

* * *

"Do you think we should try to make her muffins or pancakes or something?" Maggie asked as she searched through the pantry for ideas and supplies.

"How about we start with just coffee?" Zoe suggested. She filled the pot with water.

"How about I make breakfast so you three don't burn the house down?" Claire said, still putting on her robe as she came down the steps.

"You don't have to." Zoe was still worried about her aunt. Claire looked fine. Her hair was pulled up in a messy bun. Her eyes were bright and free of dark circles. But she had just lost someone she loved. They all had, but it was different for Claire. There had to be something mangled underneath her fresh exterior.

"Zo, I'm fine," Claire assured her and smiled, "well, mostly fine. I promise." She pulled a pan out and set it on the stove, and then turned to the fridge. "I am for sure fine enough to make bacon and eggs."

"Yay! Pity eggs!" Maggie squealed as she bounced onto the bar stool next to Daniel.

"Not pity eggs," Claire corrected, setting down the carton. "More like, time-to-kick-some-butt eggs."

"I like the sound of that," Daniel said, raising his juice glass in a toast to the idea.

Zoe was glad to see Claire in better spirits. She really was. It just wasn't what she had expected. "Are you sure you're ready for another fight?" she asked. "You...you died." Saying the words did it. That was the real issue. Losing Michael, worrying about Claire losing Michael, those were merely the surface concerns of Zoe's own turmoil. For a brief moment, she had lost Claire. She had watched her aunt bleed out on the ground, and she couldn't shake that image from her thoughts. She was the one who wasn't fine, not completely.

Claire set down her whisk, walked around the counter and hugged Zoe. "I know. I know yesterday was awful for all of us," she said. "I'm not pretending it wasn't, really. I'm not dead—but neither is Abaddon. He won't wait for us to be ready—not again— so we have to be. Now."

Zoe pulled away and wiped her eyes. "And you can fight? After what happened?"

"I'm okay," Claire replied. "I told you before that I would go into Hell itself for you. That hasn't changed. If it's possible, I feel stronger than before." Claire returned to the stove and her scrambling.

Zoe knew Claire was right. Abaddon wouldn't wait to come at them again, and getting lost in fear would only serve to strengthen the Destroyer's position. They didn't need that. He would be ready for Zoe next time. They no longer had a trump card to play. "So what do we do?" she asked her aunt.

"First, we eat a good breakfast," Claire said. She dropped bacon into the skillet, and it began to sizzle. "Then, we make Abaddon come to us. I'm tired of him choosing the fields of battle."

"I, for one, like that plan," Zoe agreed. She had just begun to pull plates from the cabinet when she suddenly noticed that the only sound in the room was the sizzling bacon. She turned back around, unsure and a little concerned at what might be happening.

The whole kitchen had stopped. Everyone was frozen in place. No one made a sound. They just stared at his smirking face. *Lucas.* He was just there—same tousled hair and mischievous grin, standing in front of them.

"Y-you all see him too, right?" Maggie stuttered.

"Yes, we do," Claire replied, a smile growing on her face. She stepped away from the stove and wrapped Lucas in a hug.

"Garrett sent me," Lucas told Claire. "He said to tell Zoe he loved her more than she would ever know, and to tell you not to worry, bird. Help would be here whenever she needed it."

Claire wiped a tear from her eye. "He sent you back in his place?" she asked him.

Lucas nodded. "He said I deserved to have my life back more than he did. Something about already having had more happiness than most, a chance to live well..."

Lucas wasn't really talking to Zoe, but she heard the message loud and clear. She felt it in her bones how much her father loved her. She missed him and her mom. She would have been elated for him to have been the one standing in that kitchen again, but she understood why he had let it be Lucas. That selflessness was another reason Zoe loved her father so very much.

"That sounds like Garrett," Claire said wiping her eyes again. "I'm sure you could eat and don't want burnt bacon, so..." She gestured for him to sit and returned to her cooking.

"I thought he was supposed to be getting reinforcements. One snarky guy seems a little underwhelming," Daniel teased. He had already stood from his chair. He gave Lucas a fist bump and bro-hug.

"I am more than awesome enough, thank you very much," Lucas responded, "and you know you missed me."

"I know I did," Zoe interrupted. She stepped up to give Lucas a hug of her own. It was hesitant at first. She needed to be sure he was real, that this wasn't some group hallucination or something. It wasn't the first time someone in her life had come back from the dead, but it was still no less unsettling. It was weird to suddenly have him right there with them after all the tears and grief and pain. Part of her was afraid it wouldn't be true, and then it would feel like losing him all over again.

"I'm really here," Lucas whispered when she squeezed him a little tighter, as if he'd read her thoughts.

"Just needed to be sure." Zoe let him go.

She had barely broken free from the embrace when Maggie leaped in, nearly shoving her out of the way to jump into Lucas's arms. "If you ever do that to me again, I will kill you."

"That's not really a threat because I'd already be dead," Lucas choked out like he was struggling to breathe through Maggie's tight clasp.

"I'm not just talking about the dying—though that's a no-no. I'm talking about the reckless heroics and jumping in front of swords and such. None of that. You are on rock formation protocol from now on, mister." Maggie still hadn't relinquished her hold.

"Rock formation protocol?" Lucas asked over Maggie's shoulder.

"It's a long story," Daniel said and patted Lucas on the back.

Zoe helped peel Maggie off of Lucas. "Are those time-to-kick-some-butt eggs about ready?" she asked. "Now we have *two* hungry boys to feed."

Lucas was finally able to take his seat at the bar. He snagged a piece of bacon off the plate, mumbling, "Real hungry."

* * *

"This is weird," Lucas said, standing in front of the small wooden cross Charlie had carved to mark his burial plot in the field by the barn. Zoe had to agree. It must be awkward standing over your own grave.

Next to it was the fresh dirt covering the grave where the other descendants had buried Michael just after dawn. Claire had paused there momentarily but then just went inside the barn without a word about it. Zoe didn't push. She assumed whatever Claire needed to say to Michael, or whatever she had needed to do to make a proper goodbye, had been done and said the night before. Today Claire was in battle mode and that was fine with Zoe because another battle was coming.

"You wanted to see it," Zoe reminded Lucas as they, along with Daniel and Maggie, headed inside to join the others in making battle preparations.

"So, do these others know about me? What I was?" Lucas asked when they reached the door.

"Since when do you care what other people think?" Daniel asked raising an eyebrow.

"You're right. I don't," Lucas replied. He smiled and slid the wooden doors open and proclaimed, "Good morning, sunshines. Who's ready to kill the devil?"

Zoe tried not to laugh when the whole room turned to look at them. There were a couple of whispers and some muttering. They hadn't talked about Lucas much, mostly because it was too painful. But there had been enough bits shared here and there that she was sure they could put the pieces together enough to know who the sarcastic kid in the black t-shirt was.

"Lucas?" The question, more like a confused realization, came from Charlie. He had been standing next to Claire but was now walking cautiously forward. Zoe wasn't sure if Claire had told him and maybe he didn't believe it until he saw Lucas, or if Claire had simply kept silent to let him be surprised.

"If it isn't my favorite grumpy old man," Lucas said. "I have to admit, I'm surprised you're not in a wheelchair—or dead."

"Now I don't know if I want to smack ya or hug ya, so yep, it's definitely you all right." Charlie grabbed Lucas and pulled him into a bear hug. "Don't go dying on us again," he said.

"Don't worry, I put him on rock formation protocol," Maggie chimed in as she skipped past them toward the archery targets.

Charlie frowned and scratched his chin. "Do I want to know?"

"No," Zoe answered.

They spent a few minutes introducing Lucas to the others. Explanations were short. If the other descendants had questions, they didn't ask them. It wasn't the time to get lost in the details of journeys through Heaven or explanations of Garrett and Lucas and how any of this was. Zoe would love nothing more than to sit on her sofa and talk to Lucas about her father. To ask if he had met her mother. She wished she could spend the day hanging out with her friends, celebrating their reunion. Instead they would stand around a table and lay out their assault on Hell's armies.

"You think he'll show up here?" Levi asked after they had thoroughly mapped out their options.

"Abaddon will be angry," Claire replied. "He'll be scared, but he'll think I'm dead and not want to wait until the mourning is over to strike. He'll come."

They had a plan. Beyond that, Zoe had confidence in something unseen. She had suffered a lot in the past few months. There were still lacerations on her soul where she could feel sadness, fear, and regret trying to break through. They might always be there, but she was learning to deal with them. She was able to cope with the twinges because she wasn't alone. She didn't carry the burden of defeating the Destroyer. She didn't even have to carry herself. Zoe sat on the steps to the loft watching her family, new faces scattered in among the now familiar. Billy and Bobby were helping newbies prepare weapons. Thomas and Catherine knelt in a corner, praying with who she assumed was Reverend Larson. Sue and Jack held hands while they sat at the table drinking coffee. Claire, Levi, and Charlie were still talking about what was soon to come. Lucas, Daniel, and Maggie were all laughing while Maggie showed off her newfound skills with her crossbow.

It was tense and peaceful all at the same time. Zoe had faith, but that didn't fully extinguish fear. Her life wasn't the only one being put on the line in a few hours. She knew Abaddon could be defeated, but she was concerned about how much more his defeat might cost. Her family had grown. It was still growing as even more descendants continued to arrive. They were all welcomed with smiles and cheers.

Be with us, Zoe prayed, then pushed herself up and went to greet her new brothers. At sunset, swords would raise and shadows would fall.

CHAPTER THIRTY-SEVEN

Claire stood next to Michael's grave, fully surrounded by the other descendants. The hues of dusk painted a vibrant backdrop to their solemn gathering. A prayer was said. Words of honor and respect were spoken. A cross was placed. Flowers were dropped. By all appearances, this was a simple funeral. But there were no tears, only the steely gazes of readiness hidden by the reverence of their bowed heads.

Claire felt a chill creep around their circle. "Pardon the interruption," Abaddon said as he appeared dressed in the skin of Benjamin Achan—a black suit, shirt, and silk tie. He stood among the dying grass of the field. "I wanted to pay my respects to the Armor-Bearer. I regret she and I never had the chance to be, well, closer."

Claire, who had been concealed among the small assembly, stepped into the open and confronted the beast. "Trust me, this is as close as you want me to get."

The Destroyer's face was difficult to read. His eyes squinted and his nostrils flared like he was angry and possibly confused, but his lips curled a touch upward in a sort of twisted pleasure. "Ah, the Guardian is the one in the grave. That makes twice someone has died to save you, dear Claire. Maybe you aren't as good as advertised after all."

Lucas stepped up next to Claire. "She is, and I'm pretty sure the angel would agree with me when I say we'd do it again. Because win or lose, she'd do the same for us. I bet you can't say that about your little minions," Lucas said.

"Boy—" Abaddon growled softly, then swallowed. He smoothed his tie before continuing, "I'm actually happy to see you. I'll enjoy getting the chance to kill you a second time."

"That isn't going to happen," Zoe said, coming to stand with Lucas and Claire.

"And he's right," Claire added. "When it comes down to it, we'd die for each other. No one is going to sacrifice themselves for you."

"Ha!" Abaddon laughed. He raised his hands and a prelude of hissing announced the rise of shadows as smoky bodies began clawing through the surface of the ground and swirling from all corners of the sky. "I have an entire army at my beck and call," he said smugly.

"And the moment they realize they picked the losing side," Claire said, "they'll flee and leave you to your end. They aren't loyal, they're just afraid." She pulled her sword from its sheath.

The rest of the descendants responded to her signal by spreading out in an orchestrated choreography. They each took their preordained posts at various mini arsenals where weapons had been hidden in the tall grass or under makeshift camouflage. Their positions created a planned circle with Claire and Zoe front and center of the Destroyer, where they would lead the push forward through the darkness to meet their enemy face-to-face.

The Destroyer laughed as he shed his skin to reveal the molten monster beneath. Claire heard the demons shriek in glee at the sight of their master. Praetors had been raised, and they shook the ground as they approached. The Bringers of Death—hellhounds— howled as Abaddon ordered them forth. More shadows slithered into rank and file. Finally, one last cloud of smoke circled near the Beast.

Meredith twisted into shape. "It looks like you all are sorely outnumbered," she said.

Claire seethed at the site of her killer. Part of her wanted to charge the proselyte, but she kept still, poised. She wouldn't act out of anger though it raged inside her. She knew their confrontation was inevitable, so she would be patient.

Electricity crackled above them, drawing Claire's attention.

"What was that you said about *us* being outnumbered?" Lucas asked as a host of angels, electric bodies and lightning wings, appeared hovering overhead.

"Dad didn't disappoint," Zoe whispered to Claire.

"No, he didn't," Claire said, relieved by the sight of the ethereal beings that encircled them. Each one placed their right hand on their chest and bowed their heads in unison in the direction of the descendants. Then, they drew their blades.

"No!" Abaddon roared. "This changes nothing!" His eyes blazed like fire and his own sword grew out of his hand, smoke and lava turning into a shining black metal. He raised it, and his army began to advance.

Claire felt the first earth-quaking steps of the praetors just before she saw them crossing the field toward the descendants. Suddenly, a bolt of lightning surged out of the sky and hit the ground in front of them. She watched blue flames grow upward and spread to form a wall of holy fire, separating the rock giants and hellhounds from the rest of the shadows.

"Oh, I think it changes things just a little bit," Lucas said with a chuckle.

Claire watched him flip his knife in his hand and fling it at a shadow. It hit the creature in the head causing the others to scream and charge.

"I hate it when you do that," Daniel yelled from his place beside Zoe.

"Somebody has to take the initiative in these situations, golden boy," Lucas yelled back as he sliced through another darkling.

"Boys, can we please focus?" Maggie scolded them from her place behind a nearby woodpile. "Some of us are trying to kill demons."

"At least save the trash talk for the enemy," Zoe said, then swung her sword, cutting through two demons at once.

Claire fought back to back with Zoe, the Daughter and the Armor-Bearer. They danced a fluid duet that pushed through the darkness toward the Destroyer. As they turned and lunged, striking the shadows around them, Claire could see the others doing the same. The guardians attacked from above, their power surging down in lightning strikes against the larger beasts. Some of them dove down upon the enemy, blue streaks of electricity that punched the rock giants and wrestled with the black dogs. Claire was confident in her team, her comrades. She knew she could depend on each descendant to do their part to rip through the blanket of demons in order to flank her and Zoe, protecting them so they could reach Abaddon.

"You aren't enough, little girl," Abaddon hissed.

"I don't have to be," Zoe replied.

The Destroyer bellowed with laughter. "You're already getting tired and I've just begun," he said, pointing his sword above his head. Half of the demons were pulled toward it. They became a cyclone of smoke, gnashing teeth, and flaming eyes. Their shrieks were like high-pitched thunder. Abaddon raised his other arm and dark energy drained from the demons like billowing smoke. It coursed into him. He smiled, the dying light of day glinting against his smooth volcanic fangs. The lava veins under his molten skin blazed brighter, a wave that flowed down his body and then back up, surging out of his hands like fire. The flames swirled around the tornado of shadows, peeling them back and taking the sky with them.

"He's tearing the veil!" Claire heard Thomas yell.

The rent widened further as more creatures clamored and scratched their way through.

"We need to end this," Claire said to Zoe between sword blows.

"We really do," Meredith said as she came sauntering through the swarm of demons. "I think it's time, don't you?" The proselyte drew her blade.

"You did kill me, so I think I should return the favor," Claire told her. She sliced through another shadow and then headed toward Meredith. "Zo?" she said, glancing toward her niece.

"Don't worry—I've got this," Zoe assured her. She smiled and blinked, her eyes white. The light filtered through her and out of the sword, laying waste to any shadow in front of her.

Claire returned her attention to Meredith. "Where were we?"

The proselyte didn't respond with words—she charged instead.

Claire turned her sword and brought it up, blocking Meredith's. The time for posturing was over, and she was glad of it. She was tired of the verbal sparring and ready to focus on finishing this fight.

"What, no witty commentary?" The proselyte asked, panting.

"Nope," was all Claire said as she deflected another advance and then pushed Meredith back hard.

Meredith retreated a step to regain her balance. "Aren't you curious where Alex is?" she asked, taking a dig.

"Since you brought it up, I'm guessing he's dead." Claire refused to be distracted and lunged forward.

Meredith blocked the charge. "You're cold, Claire—almost as cold as me. I'm a little proud," she said.

Claire would never have wished Alex dead. She ached at the thought of it. He deserved more. He deserved a second chance. But it had all been his choice. She wasn't responsible for him, for his death, and she couldn't think about it now. Too much was at stake to let the proselyte get inside her head. Claire pushed down regrets that were trying to come back to life. She had forgiven herself. She would keep forgiving herself as long as it took for those regrets to stay dead. She focused on her nemesis.

She was stronger than Meredith. She was faster, better with a sword. Without distraction, this fight was barely fair. It wasn't arrogance. Claire had simply done this long enough to be able to read her opponents, and this one was getting weaker. Meredith was growing more off balance with each step, and she knew it too. Her sword thrusts were angry, messy. This was no dream. There were no theatrics. Claire just needed to remain steady. She was already three steps ahead.

Meredith grunted and brought her sword over her head awkwardly. Claire blocked it, shoved Meredith backward, and then elbowed her across the jaw. When Meredith stumbled, Claire swept the proselyte's legs from underneath her. Claire was on top of her by the time she hit the ground, her knee against Meredith's chest, her sword against her neck. Meredith made a weak effort to raise her sword one last time.

"Uh uh," Lucas said, stepping on Meredith's wrist and forcing her to drop her weapon. "You're done."

"Not yet," the proselyte said as she writhed under Claire's hold. She lifted her other arm toward the nearby shadows, her fingers curling. Nothing happened. Her black eyes faded to green.

"Those demons aren't coming to help you," Lucas told her. "They don't care about you."

"And you do?" Meredith spat. Blood dribbled down her chin.

"Me? No," Lucas replied. "But someone might, someday."

"You don't have to lose today," Claire offered. "You can be free of this, of Abaddon." It was a long shot. Meredith was farther gone than even Lucas had been. Letting go of the power, starting over without it, might prove too difficult. But they would make the offer because everyone deserved to be saved. Everyone deserved a chance to make a new choice, a better choice.

"I picked my side," Meredith scoffed. Her jaw was clenched but her eyes glistened.

Claire felt sorry for her. This woman had caused her and her family so much suffering. That's what suffering did though—caused others to suffer too. It's wasn't an excuse. There were consequences to choices, even ones made out of brokenness. Besides, everyone was a little bit broken. It could make a person lash out, or it could give them empathy and the insight to forgive. Claire would always choose forgiveness, as much for herself as for Meredith. "Your side won't win," she told her.

"I'll survive. It's what I do," the proselyte declared as her eyes spiraled back to black. She pushed herself up, causing Claire's sword to slice the side of her throat. Blood began to stream out and then turned to puffs of smoke. "Rain check on you killing me," she choked out, then turned to black vapor and slipped out of Claire's grasp. She flowed through the mass of demons and away from the field.

"Should we go after her?" Lucas asked.

"No," Claire replied. When this was over, there would be time to find Meredith. Now was all about helping Zoe finish her task and close the gates.

The horde of demons had only grown thicker around them, a cloud that twisted and thrashed. Claire cut down the shadows that clawed at her, hacking through them to get to Zoe. It was hard to see in the dark but Zoe was a bright light in the middle. Her glow beamed in all directions, dissolving any demon it touched on her way to Abaddon.

"Zoe is almost there!" Claire yelled to the boys battling on either side of her.

"We need to get to her!" said Daniel who had fought his way through the fray to stand on Claire's right.

"Then let's move!" Lucas responded.

Claire felt a tap on her shoulder. "Don't forget about me!" said a familiar voice. She turned to see that Maggie had traded her bow for a sword. "What?" Maggie shrugged. "Levi said I was getting on his nerves worrying about where you all were, so he handed me this."

"You ready to use it?" Claire asked as she slashed a demon that was lunging from the side.

Maggie grinned. "I got here didn't I?" Another demon jumped

at them and Maggie stabbed it. It wasn't pretty but it got the job done.

"All right," Claire relented. She knew there was no stopping her at this point. They were surrounded. Maggie was in danger no matter where she stood or what weapon she handled. Might as well have her close by.

Lucas and Daniel pushed forward, leading the way. With knives in hand, they spun and lunged and stabbed through each demon that got in their way. Claire and Maggie followed, the four of them working together like a machine, mowing down their enemy until they were close enough to see Zoe, who had just come within reach of the Destroyer.

CHAPTER THIRTY-EIGHT

"Don't worry—I've got this," Zoe had said to Claire before closing her eyes. It had only been for a second, but the world had slowed to the rhythm of her calming heart. All of the sounds around her had been silenced by its steady beat. Zoe had listened to it, the thump inside her chest. She had synchronized her breathing to it and waited for the familiar tingle to burst out and flood her body.

The white light ran hot through her veins. She had watched it glow beneath the surface of her skin, making its way down her fingers and into the Eden Sword. Heat had blazed within her and had surrounded her, an invisible fire purifying everything it touched. It had radiated outward and the demons around her had screeched when they converged with it. They had dissolved into piles of ash at her feet. Step by step, Zoe had moved through the swarm. She hadn't flinched. She hadn't cringed when their claws grazed her skin. She had barely needed to lift her sword to break through them. The more shadows she burned past, the more of them Abaddon had thrust toward her. And the more the darkness besieged her, the brighter her light had become.

This was it. A prophecy written in a book thousands of years ago was coming to fruition. She was the Daughter. She was about to walk up to the center of all evil, to the gates of Hell. She was about to be the lock on the door. What did that mean? What was she supposed to do exactly? She wasn't sure, but if it did mean death, she was ready.

"You look confident for someone walking to their death." Abaddon glared at her as he spoke.

"I'm not scared to die," Zoe told the Beast. And she meant it.

"Everyone says that until they are right on the edge, but then they change their minds," Abaddon said as he turned his sword with a flick of his wrist and then pointed it at her. "You won't be any different."

The ground quivered as the Destroyer took a step toward Zoe. She squeezed the grip of the Eden Sword. Fear was trying to scratch its way to the surface of her mind. She beat it back with faith. She was powerful. She was chosen. She was loved. She was not alone. She thought of the Maker.

"Show me what to do," she said out loud. She could barely hear her own prayer as the hissing hoard around her intensified.

The Destroyer took another step toward her. He raised his sword high and then swung it down hard.

Zoe lifted the Eden Sword to block his blow. As the two blades clashed, the sound they made echoed across the field of battle. Abaddon brought his weapon around for another attack, but she blocked that one too and spun herself away. He growled and charged at her again. The Beast was not as clumsy or slow as one would surmise from the height and weight of his solid form. He was as strong though. It took all Zoe had, including the power that coursed inside her, to keep him from trampling her into the ground. With every thrust of her sword and twist away from his, she could feel her muscles tighten. Her lungs burned. Sweat beaded on her forehead and dripped down the sides of her face, making her hair stick to her temples.

Their swords met again. Abaddon pushed, and she slid backward, nearly falling to the ground. She wheezed and wiped her head with her sleeve. Zoe was determined not to give in. She roared and lunged back toward the Destroyer. Another attack and parry. Zoe quickened her pace and was able to surprise her enemy with a slice to his side. Lava dribbled out of the cut like blood.

Abaddon touched the wound and laughed. "It will take more than that," he said and then charged again.

Zoe grunted as their blades came into contact. Her body bent backward in a failing effort to keep Abaddon from forcing her to the ground. Just as she was about to falter, she ducked to the side, but she couldn't move clear fast enough, and the Beast's sword grazed her arm. It stung. She bit her lip and tried to ignore the pain. She needed a moment to regroup, so she backpedaled to widen the space between her and her enemy.

As she retreated, Zoe turned her head to the left and quickly scanned the panorama. The sky was a black mix of night and the darkness of demons, shot through with blue flashes of the guardians helping accentuate the difference between the two. All manner of hellish beasts shrieked and growled. The descendants still fought behind her. Zoe could hear their shouts and groans. She couldn't be sure they were all okay. Even if they all survived this, which she prayed they did, it wouldn't be without injury. She studied the wound on her arm and the red stain that continued to grow around it. Imagining her friends' bleeding wounds and torched skin made Zoe's heart beat faster. Her chest clenched. The longer this went on, the more dangerous it became for her friends, her family...for her. Time felt slower but it wasn't, and with every step Zoe took backward, with every glance and thought about the scene around her, Abaddon was marching toward her, closing ground once again.

"Zo!"

Zoe turned. Just behind her, emerging through the shadows were Claire, Daniel, Lucas, and Maggie.

"We're here," Claire called out as she fought.

They weren't the only ones. Zoe heard it then, the wind rustling through the tree tops. A voice blew with it. That voice. The voice that wasn't a voice at all but an echo inside her. It was quiet and loud, peaceful and booming. Most of all it was so clear. She knew what to do now. As suddenly as the answer had come to her, so did an easiness in her lungs and a renewed strength in her body.

Zoe smiled at Claire and the others, signaling it was time to end this.

They nodded.

She charged forward to meet the Destroyer.

The Beast sneered at her.

She was nearly within reach of him again when she stopped. The heat inside her intensified, burning away whatever fear or doubt was left inside her mind. Zoe raised the Eden Sword above her head. White light flowed out of it, out of her. It beamed into the sky, piercing the center of the demon storm until it reached the tear in the veil. Shadows began to be sucked back into the ragged gateway.

"If you think your little light show scares me, you're going to be disappointed," Abaddon's deep voice boomed. "You should have aimed for me."

"Oh, I'm not worried about you anymore," Zoe said, "and I'm not the one you should be worried about."

The Destroyer growled and reached out as if to grab her.

The wind left the trees and gathered behind Zoe. A sparkling light reflected off its edges, giving it form. It moved and roared like a mighty lion as it blew over and through her, right into the Destroyer, lifting him off the ground.

Abaddon choked, gasping for air. "You have not beaten me, girl!" he yelled as he fought futilely against the force that held him.

"*I* never needed to," Zoe said as she flipped her sword and drove it into the ground.

The Beast's granite layers crumbled under the Maker's power. The lava beneath bled out of the cracks. It bubbled up through his mouth and dripped from his fangs. The hellhounds yelped, and the shadows curled in pain. The ground shook as praetors began a haphazard retreat. The wind, its light growing ever brighter, wrapped around Abaddon, binding him. He released an agonizing scream as he was thrust through the seam just before the veil completely closed. When it did, a ripple shot from it. The demons that hadn't run were obliterated.

Another roar echoed overhead.

The guardians exited in blurs of blue light.

The descendants were left standing silent under the stars.

The wind moved around each of them before it encircled Zoe in an invisible embrace.

Then it was gone.

It was over.

CHAPTER THIRTY-NINE

The scent of bacon and coffee woke Zoe. She rubbed the sleep from her eyes. Her blankets were cozy and her bed was warm. She considered rolling over and allowing herself the luxury of another hour of rest. Her stomach growled its protest to the notion so Zoe got up. She stretched and yawned. She pulled back the edge of her white curtains and blinked at the sun's brightness. Outside, birds were whistling and a neighbor's dog was barking. Across the street, Abigail waved to her while picking up the morning paper. Zoe waved back. Downstairs, she could hear pans rattling and Claire singing along with the radio. Zoe yawned again, then grabbed the hoodie off her chair and slipped it over her head. She pulled her hair up and went to brush her teeth.

For the second time in her life, Zoe didn't recognize the reflection in the mirror. It wasn't a bad thing. Her eyes were bright and her skin glistened. There were no dark circles or sadness. This girl wasn't broken and lonely. This girl had faced the darkness and overcome it. Not just on a field of battle, but in her mind and heart.

"Zo, breakfast!" Claire called up the stairs.

"Coming!" Zoe smiled at herself then rinsed the sink. She jogged down the steps, hopping off the last one.

Claire was singing and dancing to the tune of some nineties pop song. "Good morning," she sang as she twirled herself to the end of the counter. She took Zoe by the hand and spun her around.

Plenty of sarcastic comments were on the tip of Zoe's tongue but she held them back. It seemed appropriate to dance around the kitchen after saving the world. They were celebrating life. Maybe that's why Claire did it all the time, because she already knew what Zoe was just figuring out—you have to celebrate the wins, the big ones and even the little ones. You have to find moments of joy in this life. You have to dance around the kitchen sometimes. What better day for that than today?

"This is what I'm talking about." Zoe heard Maggie's voice and turned in time to see her friend come bursting into the room with Daniel and Lucas not far behind. She immediately joined the revelry.

"May I cut in?" Daniel asked, holding his hand out to Zoe.

"You may," Claire consented. She passed Zoe off and bopped her way back to the griddle.

Zoe giggled when Maggie reached for Lucas, who jerked back and said, "Oh no, I don't dance."

"I'm with the kid," Charlie added as he walked in and pulled out a chair.

"Oh, you're both dancing," Maggie said firmly. She grabbed both their arms and pulled them to an open space.

Zoe knew they had no choice but to relent. Pretty soon their reluctant faces were smiling.

"We look ridiculous," Lucas said and laughed.

Maggie kissed his cheek. "Well, if you can't look a little ridiculous with your friends, then what's the point, right?" She giggled and twirled herself into his arms and back out again.

Zoe found it hard to believe that just yesterday they had been fighting a war. As the rest of the descendants trickled in, the kitchen became even more festive, overflowing with laughter and music and family. The song changed and breakfast was ready. They ate together and then moved their unplanned celebration into the living room. They talked about the battle. They kept singing, mostly off key. They exchanged emails and phone numbers and promised to keep in touch better than they had in the past. They designated the day an official bloodline holiday that they would celebrate every year, hopefully together. They made plans.

Zoe took a backseat to the majority of the conversation. She just watched and listened. It was awkward when someone mentioned how cool her "Zo-glow" was or asked her to recount the details of the night before. She didn't feel like she had done much. She hadn't won that battle; she had just been obedient in fighting it like they all had. She had showed up and played her part, and now it was finished.

People left the way they came in, a couple at a time. The house quieted as it emptied. Zoe found Claire in the kitchen cleaning up.

"Need some help?" she asked her aunt.

"Sure," she said and tossed Zoe the towel.

They stood at the sink, one washing and one drying.

Zoe sighed.

"That was loaded," Claire observed. She set the plate she was holding back in the sink and dried her hands before turning directly to Zoe. "What is it you're wanting to ask me?"

Zoe finished drying the glass in her hand. She set it gently on the counter. She knew the question that was circling; it had been cycling through her thoughts all day. Why couldn't she just say it? It felt selfish. It felt too simple. It felt scary. She had helped to defeat a great evil and five words were making her queasy.

"Anytime now," Claire said, interrupting Zoe's anxious inner conversation.

"What do I do now?" The words blurted out.

Claire laughed. "That's what was so hard to ask me?"

"It seems like a stupid question, but I don't know how to answer it," Zoe replied.

"It's not stupid, Zo. For the past few months, your whole life has been thrown for a loop, and your whole identity has revolved around being the Daughter and fulfilling a prophecy. Now that's done. Switching gears can be hard. But you live the same way you have for months now, like you have purpose—chosen for something great."

"Something great?" Zoe asked. "After last night, everything else just seems average."

"That's a matter of perspective, doll. The world may or may not need your sword, but I know it still needs you." Claire placed her hand on Zoe's. "Saving it isn't always about killing a 'big bad' and fending off an apocalypse. We aren't like Buffy," Claire said with a chuckle. "Your purpose is bigger and will stretch farther and last longer than just being the Daughter of the Three. You'll figure out what comes next." Claire returned to washing the dirty dishes.

Her aunt was right. They weren't just one singular thing; their lives were more complex than that. This fight was finished, but Zoe would still have a million little choices to make every day. All of them had the power to save, to change things, to change a person, a tiny bit at a time. Her identity was secure. Daughter or not, she would continue to walk around as one who is loved. That would make loving others easier. That love was the real power. It's what had saved the world, and would continue to save it day after day. She didn't know what it would always look like. She didn't need to. Sometimes you just had to show up. You had to take it one step at a time. Her next step was finishing high school.

Zoe picked up another glass to dry. "So what about you? Do you even know how to live without a sword in your hand?" she asked Claire.

Claire laughed. "Not really, but my sword might still come in handy."

"What do you mean?"

"The Destroyer is gone, but some of his poison remains," Claire replied, handing Zoe a plate.

"Like Meredith?" Zoe asked.

"Yes, and others that are still scattered on this side of the veil.

Someone's got to take down the rest of the monsters." Claire bumped her hip against Zoe's. "Don't worry though. I'm leaving clean up duty to the other descendants until after graduation. Then, if you want to join me you can, but it'll be up to you. You can do anything kid."

It had only been three months since Zoe found out the truth of who she was. Had it really been only three? That didn't feel right. It felt like a lifetime. It felt like the difference between being a child and being an adult. Zoe would be eighteen in a few weeks. She didn't have to think about anything but physics class and college applications and senior prom if she didn't want to. She could be like everyone else. In the middle of everything, that was all Zoe had ever wanted—to be ordinary, to be normal. Why? Normal was overrated. Weren't we created for more than that? Daughter of the Three or not, she was made for extraordinary things. She had been chosen, and she was going to live like it. Zoe Renee Andrews vowed never to go back to life as usual.

"But first—is there any pie left?"

EPILOGUE

The faintest bit of morning light peeked through the lush rain forest branches as Claire returned to her tent, sweaty, dirty, and tired. She had just enough water left in her canteen to wash her face, so that would have to do. She wanted to sleep, but her stomach was growling. She rifled through her pack for a protein bar and sat on the edge of her bed to eat it, wishing for something more savory. Real food could wait though. Right now her aching muscles needed rest; her mind needed it too. She picked up her tablet, hoping there was at least a little battery life left on it. She pulled up her email and read.

C,

    Thanks for the care package. I'm not sure how you even got to a post office, but because I know it couldn't have been easy. I will, at least, try these weird chocolate covered ants you sent me. Maybe the caffeine and protein will help me pass my last final.

    I've been stuck in this library studying all day and will actually be thankful to go hunt some demons with Daniel tonight.

    Lucas says hi, and not to kill everything before he gets there.

Our flight leaves on Sunday. Maggie is coming along after all. She told her parents the truth. They didn't believe her at first. You can't blame them though. I let her show them the book. I think they're still processing it all but it's near impossible to say no to Mags when she gets her heart set on something. Right now her heart is set on cheering you up because she is sure you are at least a little bit mopey still. Prepare yourself.

I can't decide if this first college semester went by really slowly or too fast. I miss you though. I can't wait to see you and spend Christmas together, even if it's in the middle of the jungle.

Love,

Z

PS: Maggie says to tell Charlie she was serious in the letter she sent him and he had better have gotten some decorations together. She tried and failed to fit a small artificial tree in her suitcase so she is not joking about this.

Claire had read the same saved email at least ten times already, but it still made her laugh. Between the retellings of college shenanigans and the wonderful balance of snarky Lucas and perky Maggie quotes, most of Zoe's emails made her laugh. They hadn't seen each other since August when Claire had helped her unpack her dorm room. Well, except that one FaceTime call, but it only lasted five minutes before the Wi-Fi connection went wonky. That's the trouble with traveling abroad, especially when that travel has you spending most of your time so far from a decent cell signal, you feel like you've gone back in time.

Claire had been slaying her way through South America with Charlie and Levi for the past three months. The two men had been following signs of demonic activity ever since the closing of the veil. The demons, praetors, and hellhounds that weren't destroyed had scattered all over the world, and they were scared and hungry which made for a dangerous combination. They had called her when they came across a particularly nasty infestation below the equator. As soon as Zoe was settled, Claire had come, and one village at a time, they had either killed the shadows present or had driven them out. This was the Armor-Bearer's life post prophetic battle.

Last night had been no different. As soon as the sun had sunk below the horizon, Claire had strapped on her sword and began her patrol of the village's perimeter. The indigenous people had become so afraid of the creatures they could feel but could not see, creatures that stalked them in the darkness, that they had begun retreating into their huts just before dark. Their laughter and music would grow silent and their fires would be put out, replaced by the red glow of demon eyes and the shrill hiss of shadows. Claire hunted the monsters. She fought them. She killed them.

Claire also had another enemy to fight—her own grief. The emails from Zoe helped. Back in Torch Creek, Zoe and the others had kept Claire focused. They had given her a reason to push through the mourning. Here in the jungle, Charlie and Levi were good company, but she was often alone. It wasn't like before when she had been so forlorn and resentful. Claire had learned the art of living at peace, but peace didn't mean the absence of regret or loneliness. Choosing peace merely helped her hold those hungrier emotions at a distance, which made them bearable. Unfortunately, fatigue often became the door that let those feelings back in. Claire wouldn't allow them to totally overtake her again, but she couldn't always keep them completely away. She missed him. The last time she'd lived this life, he had been a part of it. Living like this again further uncloaked the void his death had left.

Claire set down the tablet and half-eaten protein bar. She turned the pearl bracelet on her wrist and then lay down on her cot. She closed her eyes and listened as the village woke up. Children laughed and the women sang as they began the new day. It was a glorious noise to fall asleep to.

"Claire!" Charlie yelled from outside the tent.

Her body told her to ignore him. He didn't sound panicked or threatened. Couldn't whatever it was wait for her to rest?

The flap of her tent folded open, and Levi peeked in. "You're going to want to come out here," he said.

"Okay," she moaned. She sat up and rubbed the back of her neck before stretching her way to her feet. She poked her head out of the tent and blinked at the now bright sky. She raised her hand, trying to block the glare.

Charlie and Levi's silhouettes began to take colorful shape as she fully emerged from her shelter. She followed their gazes down the path and saw a figure walking toward them. It appeared to be a man—a tall, strong man.

"Michael?" She gasped his name. It couldn't be, could it?

Claire stepped cautiously forward. The closer she got, the more his features came into focus. The statuesque outline of his body. The hair that brushed his shoulders. The line of his jaw. His blue eyes. They weren't exactly the same. They didn't have that startling supernatural luminescence they'd had before, but they were still brighter than the average blue eyes. His smile was just a little different too. It seemed more natural—more real.

"Hello." His voice was the same deep tone that resonated inside her.

"How are...?" She slid her palm against his cheek. Her fingers briefly played with a strand of his hair.

Michael took her hand and moved it to his chest, and his heart beat against it. "I am alive but not the same," he told her.

"You're human now," she said, understanding. How was this real? Why? The questions were there but Claire didn't care to ask them out loud. The answers didn't really matter. Her soul already screamed the answer deep within. *The Maker did this.*

"A gift." Michael wiped a fresh tear from her cheek with his thumb. He cradled her face in his hands and drew her close. His lips crashed against hers in a long-awaited kiss.

The end...and the beginning.

ACKNOWLEDGMENTS

Writing a book is hard. I think it's even harder to put it out into the world. It's a very vulnerable thing to create a story that is one hundred percent your own and then let other people into it. I don't think I would have been brave enough without the awesome demon slayers around me.

Allison, Victoria, Bryanna, Adelaide, and Eleanor, thanks for loving this story and for believing in it, and me, from the very beginning. You will always be my most favorite fangirls and friends. (One of these days I'm going to share your awesome and hilarious fangirl-ranting TCO3 emails with the world because the world needs to experience them.)

Meagan, Aly, and Kelly, thank you for being a support to me. You have blessed me in so many ways. You have no idea what you have meant to me. I have loved talking with you about these books, and publishing, and life. I feel lucky to have you as friends.

Emerald, Kara, Heather, Becki, Jacqueline, Laura, Guy, Melissa, and all the other slayers on my squad, you all rock socks! You have kept me going on days I wanted to quit and for that I am beyond grateful.

Amanda, Sherry, and Stephanie, thanks for taking on these

books and me. I tried really hard not to be some diva author, I swear I did. This industry can be brutal, but Blue Ink has been like a family. One that I am proud to be a part of. (Shout out to Christa for jumping right into my manic writer/marketing nonsense from literally her first day at Blue Ink.)

Holly, thanks for being my bestie and for always having my back and for being someone I can be my genuine, weird self with.

Mom and Dad, thanks for being my biggest cheerleaders and for working overtime to sell my books to all your friends. You have always made me feel like I could do anything.

To my daughters, Lila and Rory, thanks for letting mommy write this book even when you wanted to play, for being a very loud and sassy soundtrack to most of it, and for thinking it was cool that I wrote a book. I love you heaps.

To Brian, thank you for being the kind of husband that lets his wife dream big, and who helps hold those dreams up when they get heavy and she gets tired. I love you…*more*.

To all those who have read this and loved it and been encouraged and inspired by it, thank you. It is my privilege to be even this small part of your life. (If you didn't love it, I still appreciate you reading it, and maybe you'll like the next thing I write. But we're cool if you don't. You can't please everyone after all.) To DG64, watch out for the demon juice.

Most of all, thanks to the Maker, the Lover of my soul. Everything I do is because of and for You. I hope my life makes you happy.

To all the demon slayers out there, you are stronger than the darkness. You are powerful, chosen, loved, and never alone. I believe that so deep in my bones. I hope that you believe it about yourself. (If you don't, start with the Maker. He will help.) Don't give up. Keep fighting.

With Love and Lollipops,

Tabitha

PS: I love you all more than pie and that's saying something.

ABOUT THE AUTHOR

Tabitha Caplinger is a wife, mom, youth pastor, and professed tv addict. It's seriously a problem but she doesn't plan on getting help anytime soon. Mostly because she loves the stories. She can't help but get lost in the worlds created and invested in the lives of the characters. She brings that same passion for the story to her own writing. She is the author of *The Chronicle of the Three: Bloodline* and *The Chronicle of the Three: Armor-Bearer*. Aside from writing and watching tv, Tabitha can be found singing off key and dancing in the kitchen or car with her two adorably sassy daughters and awesome husband who she thinks is kind of cute.

Tabitha loves to connect with her readers! Find her on social media or at www.tabithacaplinger.com